To all the lovely kids and teachers
I had the pleasure of accompanying on the
2022 PGL trip to Windmill Hill – thank you
for the inspiration but not so much the
lack of sleep!

A special shout-out to Ella and Mia, who keep
pestering me to dedicate a book to them – your
perseverance has finally paid off. ☺

LOTTIE BROOKS'S TOTALLY DISASTROUS SCHOOL TRIP

KATIE KIRBY

PUFFIN

PUFFIN BOOKS

UK | USA | Canada | Ireland | Australia
India | New Zealand | South Africa

Puffin Books is part of the Penguin Random House group of companies
whose addresses can be found at global.penguinrandomhouse.com.

www.penguin.co.uk　　　www.puffin.co.uk　　　www.ladybird.co.uk

Penguin
Random House
UK

First published 2023
001

The brands mentioned in this book are trademarks belonging to third parties

Text design by Kim Musselle
Printed and bound in Great Britain by Clays Ltd, Elcograf S.p.A.

The authorized representative in the EEA is Penguin Random House Ireland,
Morrison Chambers, 32 Nassau Street, Dublin D02 YH68

A CIP catalogue record for this book is available from the British Library

ISBN: 978-0-241-56205-5

All correspondence to:
Puffin Books
Penguin Random House Children's
One Embassy Gardens, 8 Viaduct Gardens, London SW11 7BW

WEDNESDAY 24 AUGUST

So when I said I was a 'bit' sunburnt I may have been playing it down.

I basically look like a tomato/lobster/strawberry/clown's nose/angry spot/VERY, VERY red thing. It's all the sun's fault – I'm so cross at it!

Mum keeps going 'I hate to say I told you so . . .' and Dad and Toby keep making jokes like this . . .

TOBY:	Do you think Lottie would make a good librarian when she's older?
DAD:	Well, she's certainly well RED!
BOTH:	HA HA HAAAAAAAA.

They are like SO hilarious. URGH.

I've tried covering myself with aftersun, which does feel nice and cool, but it's not doing very much to help with the redness. I'm basically going to have to hide at home until my skin returns to a normal non-fire-engine shade.

OOH, hang on – my phone just pinged.

> Amber created group
> 'The Queens of Eight Green'

> Amber added you

AMBER: EEEEEEEEEK! Welcome to our new WhatsApp, guys!! I've just realized that we have TWO weeks until we go back to school! Now we are all back in a gang, we should have as much fun as is humanly possible. Any ideas?!?

POPPY: OOOH good plan! How about we go shopping for new pencil cases?

AMBER: Err . . . no.

MOLLY: You could come over to mine and we could paint our toenails? I have this really cute pastel-green colour I'm dying to try out.

AMBER: Also no.

JESS: We could go to the library and read all our English texts for next year. 🤓

AMBER: MAJOR NO! Guys, come on – think BIG! Brighton is our lobster.

ME: Well, I can't do anything because I have sunburn and am an actual lobster. 🦞

AMBER: Oh, come on! Don't exaggerate, Lottie. It can't be that bad!

ME: I'm not exaggerating. I'm like literally on fire!

JESS: If you were literally on fire, you wouldn't be on WhatsApp casually telling us you were on fire.

ME: It's like a tiny face fire, so maybe I would?!

JESS: Is 'a tiny face fire' the official medical condition?

ME: Probably!

AMBER: If you guys have had enough of this boring, pointless conversation then can we get back to more important issues like HAVING FUN?!

ME: How can I have fun when I look like this . . .

POPPY: OMG. You've turned into a fire engine?!?

ME: NO! I mean that's the colour of my skin.

JESS: Eek – that is pretty bad . . .

ME: Told you!

JESS: Shame you aren't an actual fire engine though, as then you could put your own tiny face fire out!

ME: True 😥

AMBER: Right, well sorry about your face fire, Lottie, but if we've finally finished chatting nonsense then maybe the rest of us (who don't look like fire engines) can make plans? Let's meet at Starbucks tomorrow at 11 a.m. and we can brainstorm?

JESS: Yay – the Frappuccinos are on me!

MOLLY: Whoop!

POPPY: Can't wait xx

ME: Well, have fun, I guess . . .

JESS: Just to be clear – I was only joking. I can't afford to buy everyone Frappuccinos (sadly) . . .

WOW. Well, that majorly sucks. I can't believe everyone is going and having fun without me – you'd have thought they'd have a bit more sympathy! I'll just have to cross everything that my tiny face fire is much better tomorrow.

THURSDAY 25 AUGUST

Woke up and looked in the mirror expecting a massive improvement, but I still look pretty fire-engine-ish so I'm stuck at home while all my friends are out having Frappuccinos.

WHY IS LIFE SO UNFAIR?!?!??!

6.34 p.m.

More bad news: Mum has just informed me that she and Dad are going out tomorrow evening, so even the Fun Police have a better social life than me!!

Worse still, despite me being *almost* thirteen, we are still getting a BABYSITTER!

I tried to convince Mum that I would be totally fine looking after Bella and Toby on my own, but she reminded me of the time when I was supposed to be

watching them while she had a bath, and she came back
into the living room to find this . . .

I said, 'Why do you have to keep going on about that?! It
was **ONE TIME!**'

'Well, what about the time when I asked you to keep
Toby amused while I made an important phone call, and
he ended up ordering £150 worth of Domino's Pizza with
MY credit card?'

'OK . . . two times . . . It's hardly like I –'

'What about the time that –'

'OK, OK – I get your point! Jeez.'

'Great. Well, that's settled then. Jean is coming over at 7.30 p.m.'

'OH GOD. Not Old Jean the Mean Machine!'

'Lottie, that is very rude. She is not that old and she's certainly not a Mean Machine, whatever that is supposed to be. Plus, it's not OK to give people derogatory nicknames!'

'Why not?! People give me derogatory nicknames ALL the time!'

'LOTTIE!'

THOUGHT OF THE DAY:

I mean, I know Mum might not agree, but that time when Toby spent £150 at Domino's was EXCELLENT. We had pizza for dinner every night for a whole week, which meant we had a brief respite from her VOM cottage pie. Even Dad was secretly delighted.

FRIDAY 26 AUGUST

1.35 p.m.

Woe is me. So much is wrong in my life . . .

1. Still look like a fire engine, but now also
   have bits of skin peeling off my nose and
   forehead, so I look like a fire engine with
   dandruff.

2. My father and brother are still the most
   irritating and unfunny people on the
   planet . . .

TOBY: Would you like to have Lottie's life, Dad?
DAD: Not really – it doesn't look very APPEALING!

3. Am still stuck indoors while my friends are
   going shopping without me (rude).

4. Am getting babysat by Old Jean the Mean
   Machine. (I don't care what MUM says – it's

true. She is mean! Last time she was here she confiscated my phone and tried to teach me how to knit.)

(5.) Mum and Dad are actually all mushy with each other and going on about how much fun their 'Date Night' will be. I don't think parents should be able to go out without their children. I mean, imagine thinking it's OK to outsource them to somebody else because you can't be bothered to look after them – ESPECIALLY a Mean Machine!

(6.06 p.m.)

I'm writing this sitting in my parents' bedroom while they get ready. I am doing my best most miserable face and they've not even offered to cancel their Date Night!

(6.14 p.m.)

They are acting all excited and chatting to each other in cheerful voices.

It's **SO** cringe. I prefer it when they are arguing about how to stack the dishwasher properly.

(6.22 p.m.)

They have put some music on and now they are dancing! **URGH!**

(6.34 p.m.)

OMG, they just kissed!

I mean, I'm RIGHT HERE on their bed, and they literally did that in front of me!

I had to make a vomiting noise to interrupt them, or God knows what might have happened.

If Mum gets pregnant again, I'm moving out!!

7.47 p.m.

The Mean Machine is here. She turned the TV off because it's 'bad for our eyes' and is forcing me and Toby to play Snakes and Ladders. If I so much as look at my phone, she tuts and says things like, 'In my day, families used to actually interact with each other.' She's also forced me to make her five trillion cups of tea while she sits on the sofa with her feet up because her bunions are aching.

7.59 p.m.

GROSS – she asked if I could rub her bunions! I said I couldn't because I have a foot phobia, and she said that the only way to get over phobias is to expose yourself to them more often – and then she shoved her right foot

right in my face AND her toe almost went up my nostril.
Oh my life – the smell! It was like a mix of cheese and
lavender; I was actually gagging, so I had to excuse
myself to go to the toilet.

8.11 p.m.

Just hiding in the toilet really to avoid the bunions. Quite
bored. Maybe she'll fall asleep soon and then I can hijack
the TV and get my phone back. Fingers crossed.

8.14 p.m.

OMG, Jean knocked on the toilet door and said it was
time for me and Toby to go to bed. Like, at the same
time!! I tried to tell her that Toby is four years younger
than me and that my normal bedtime at the weekend is
10 p.m. and she said that she didn't believe me and if I
kept telling porky-pies I'd grow a long nose like Pinocchio.
Not only that but she made me leave my phone
downstairs too. What on earth am I meant to do now?!

At least I don't have to rub any bunions, I guess . . .

Wow, who would have thought it? I've actually been quite productive without my phone! I've tidied my room, completed my English homework, filed my nails, done twenty-seven lunges (right side only as I got bored) and daydreamed about being one of Taylor Swift's backing dancers (epic). Oh, and I've also researched bunion-prevention techniques. Apparently picking up small objects with your toes is a good exercise to do, so I snuck downstairs to the kitchen, grabbed a box of Weetos and emptied them over my bedroom floor. Get this – not only can I pick them up off the floor but I can also feed myself them directly from my foot like some sort of wizard!

Bella has woken up. The Mean Machine has the TV on so loud (is it not bad for YOUR eyes then, Jean?!) that she hasn't even heard her – great babysitting . . . **NOT!** I've had to bring Bella into my room and the only way I can stop her crying is to give her the floor Weetos. She seems to like them a lot better than her jarred baby food, that's for sure.

10.32 p.m.

Oh dear. We have eaten ALL the Weetos and I am now having to let her hold the hamsters (and when I say 'hold', I mean 'squeeze to death').

11.15 p.m.

Thank goodness the Fun Police are back. Bella was just about to eat Fuzzball the 3rd!

Jeez, you try to do a good thing and all you get is complaints . . .

Mum and Dad are now upset with me for eating an entire box of Weetos at ten o'clock at night. I tried to explain that:

A. It was actually 10.14 p.m.

B. It was actually Bella who ate most of them.

C. We were actually eating them with our feet to prevent bunions.

17

But apparently those things just made it worse, and they don't even care about our long-term foot health! Instead, they think I shouldn't be feeding Bella sugary chocolate cereal when she is only nine months old.

I think they shouldn't go out and leave us with a substandard babysitter who tries to poke her bunions in my face.

I guess we will have to agree to disagree.

SATURDAY 27 AUGUST

Bad news: Mum is still cross. It didn't help that Bella refused to eat her organic porridge and blueberries for breakfast and kept trying to grab my Coco Pops.

Good news: my sunburn has finally disappeared – **WHOOP!**

My skin is still a little flaky though, so I put loads of Mum's expensive face cream on to help stick the flakes back down. I may look a bit greasy but that's better than being red . . . I think?!

I'm going to meet the girls at the park for a picnic and it's going to be so good being FREE again. This must be what it feels like when you get out of prison, but slightly better, I imagine.

6.54 p.m.

First, I met Jess at Sainsbury's Local to get picnic items. Mum gave me a fiver to buy something 'healthy and filling', which sounded boring, so I ended up getting a bag of Jelly Belly beans, a six-pack of Monster Munch and some Hubba Bubba, which seemed like a nutritious meal to me. The Monster Munch were pickled-onion flavour, so they tick the carbohydrate and vegetable box (I think).

My choices were healthier than Jess's anyway, as she spent her fiver on a massive bottle of orangeade, five packets of strawberry laces and *Heat* magazine!

When we arrived at the park, Amber, Molly and Poppy were already there, sprawled out over a large fleecy picnic blanket covered in a watermelon pattern.

'Aha – speak of the devil!' said Amber, as we settled ourselves down on the picnic blanket. 'Would you like some pink lemonade?'

'Yes please,' I said, suddenly realizing how thirsty I was.

She opened up a cute pink cool box and poured some delicious-looking fizz from a bottle into a plastic wine glass and then added a few cubes of ice. Amber always has the fanciest stuff.

'Thanks,' I said, taking a sip. 'It's delicious.'

'Yeh, it's from Harrods or somewhere posh like that. My mum gets it delivered.'

'Wow, you are SO lucky,' said Jess, who had already downed most of hers.

'Yeh, well whatever,' said Amber, looking bored. 'Anyway, we were just talking about you, Lottie.'

I frowned. I didn't like the thought of them discussing me when I wasn't there.

Amber went on. 'Poppy was telling us all about your holiday romance with your HFB . . . What was his name again?'

I scowled at Poppy, because that was private. If I had wanted Amber to know about my Handsome French Boy, I would have told her myself.

Poppy looked down guiltily and fiddled with her shoelaces. 'Sorry, Lottie . . . It kind of slipped out . . . accidentally . . .'

'Why are you sorry?' Amber piped up. 'Lottie doesn't mind, do you? I want to hear all about it!'

I sighed. 'It's fine. I just didn't want *everyone* to know . . .'

'**OOOOH**, I get it – because of Daniel, right?!' said Amber.

'No, well . . . maybe, I –'

'Look,' Amber said, interrupting me. 'We aren't going to tell Daniel, are we, girls?'

I could feel my cheeks getting hot, and it wasn't the after-effect of the sunburn. 'There is nothing to tell! Nothing happened and anyway . . . I'm not sure what's going on with Daniel.'

'Poppy said you kissed him before you went on holiday!' added Amber.

What?! I gave Poppy another scowl.

'Ooops!' she said meekly.

I felt really cross with her, but I suppose I hadn't specifically told her not to say that either.

'Well, it was just a little –' I began.

'That's so **EXCITING!**' shrieked Amber.

I blushed a little bit. I guess it was kind of nice to have the attention for once.

'It is exciting,' said Molly, looking kind of sad. 'I just can't believe you didn't tell me . . .'

Oh God. Why hadn't I told my oldest friend my biggest news?! I felt terrible.

'I'm sorry,' I blurted. 'It was right before I went away, and you were on holiday too, and then we were so busy with Jess's birthday and . . . I was only waiting for the right time. I promise.'

'It's OK,' Molly said, smiling. 'I get it . . . but, Lottie, it all sounds a bit of a mess. You have both an HFB and Daniel interested in you?!'

'Don't forget Bailey!' said Jess, laughing.

'Who is Bailey?!' said Molly.

'OH GOD!' I said, putting my head in my hands. 'It's a long story . . .'

And then I told them everything . . . I think I'd had my head in the sand until now, because suddenly I started to feel quite nervous about it all.

MONDAY 29 AUGUST

OOOOOOHHHHHH something interesting has happened!

I've had an email from Antoine. I was quite surprised because, although we swapped deets, I had kind of assumed he wouldn't get in touch. I was pleased though, especially since the email really made me laugh . . .

> From: Antoine Roux
> To: Lottie Brooks
> Subject: I love cheese
>
> Chère Lottie,
>
> How is your lovely self? I have been thinking of you every singular second of the day since we departed from the village of tents and so I ask my extremely good-looking brother, Hugo, to translate you an email from me. I hope you will find it mildly offensive.

So, let us begin! It was a wonder time when your plastic forks fell to the ground and I collected them. It was even more of a wonder time when we took a cheesy nature walk. Every time I eat a piece of Brie I think of your fine facial features.

I must make confessions that my eyes did have a crying situation when you never reply to my letter asking if you could be the girl friend of Antoine ☹ Is it because I smell of BO?

Well, whatever your reasons, I do believe you could be the material of an average girlfriend. However, I do not want to scare you away by being too obsessed. So firstly, let our personalities be shown to one another. I would like to force you to answer me some deeply personal questions . . .

1. If you could be a dog or a duck, which one would you choose?

2. What would you like to be when you grow into a large human with responsible hands?

3. If you could only pick one cheese for the
rest of your everlasting life, which would it
be? Do not say the cheddar variety, as that is
a disgrace to French people.

4. An easy one to finish. What is the meaning
of life?

That is enough for one email I should think.
I hope Hugo has translated it well. He really
is VERY good-looking. For some reason my
family genes make me look like a teapot.

Love of Antoine x

I am beginning to suspect that Hugo is playing a cruel
trick on Antoine and purposely translating things badly!

I thought about replying right away, but then decided
that I didn't want him to know that I had nothing better
to do than immediately reply to emails (even though I
don't). I would prefer that he thought I was out horse
riding or javelin throwing or skateboarding (even though
I'm not . . . and even though I have no interest in any of
those things).

12.17 p.m.

TQOEG WhatsApp group:

ME: OMG, I got an email from the HFB!!!!!!!!!!!!!!!!

AMBER: OMGEEEEEEEEEEEEEEEE!

POPPY: OOOOOMMMMMMMMGGGGGGGGGGG!

MOLLY: OHHHH MMMMMMMMMYYYY GGGGGGGAAAAWWWD!

JESS: Can everybody stop OMGing so much? It makes us sound like silly squealy schoolgirls!

POPPY: Errr, we are silly squealy schoolgirls?

JESS: Good point – OMG, what did it say????

29

ME: Well, it was a bit strange. I'm not sure his English is particularly great, but he did say that he thinks about me when he eats cheese AND he asked me to be his girlfriend again!

AMBER: WOW! Are you gonna say yes???

ME: I'm not sure . . . I'm still a bit confused about how I feel about Daniel.

POPPY: Who cares about Daniel when you could go out with an HFB?

ME: But it's not like I'm ever gonna see Antoine though, is it?

MOLLY: That's the best thing about it – you can tell everyone that you have a Hot French Boyfriend and you don't even have to worry about fitting him into your busy schedule.

ME: WOW that is clever! Maybe I'll see what the situ is like on Monday with D and decide then.

ME: Oh – one more thing – would you guys prefer to be a dog or a duck?

AMBER: Dog for sure. They get to live in nice warm houses and get tummy tickles.

POPPY: But if you were a dog, you'd have to eat dog food . . .

AMBER: But if you were a dog, you'd like eating dog food . . .

JESS: Duck. They can fly – and flying looks EXTRA MEGA COOL!

MOLLY: Plus ducks do a super-cute waddly walk!

ME: Hmmm . . . This is deffo a tough call, but I'm gonna go dog because ducks must get cold bums from sitting on a pond all day and I hate having a cold bum.

JESS: Just tried to find a cold-bum emoji but there isn't one 🤣

TUESDAY 30 AUGUST

It turned out that I didn't have to wait too long to see
Daniel. Me and the girls were lying on the beach trying
to top up our tans before school, when we saw him
and Theo approaching. They were on their way to Hove
Lagoon where they were going to have a wakeboarding
lesson.

One minute I was happily flicking through a magazine,
and the next I hear Poppy say, 'Oh, look, there's Theo and
Daniel.'

PANIC!

I looked up and saw them striding towards us, smiling,
tanned and happy. I didn't know how I was meant to
act. It was really awkward as I hadn't texted Daniel back
about meeting up and I didn't want anyone opening their
big mouths about Antoine.

I quickly whispered to the girls, 'No one mention anything about my HFB!'

'Ooooh, so he's *your* HFB now, is he? I thought you were *just friends . . .*' teased Amber.

God, why does she have to be so annoying?!

'We are! You know what I mean . . . Just don't say –'

It was too late to finish my sentence. They were here.

We all waved and said hi. I noticed that Daniel's hair had grown longer and was flopping into his eyes. He looked good. I suddenly felt pretty shy, as I always do when I bump into people I've not seen for a while. Especially when those people are **BOYS** and ESPECIALLY when they are **BOYS I HAVE KISSED!**

'How were your holidays?' Theo asked us all.

I was about to answer, but Amber got in there first. 'Mine was pretty good, thanks, but not as good as Lottie's!' she said with a big grin.

WHAT THE HELL?!

Daniel looked at me, smiling. 'Oh, really – what happened on your holiday?'

'I, er . . . um, nothing . . . I –'

'She met a really cute French dude, and he wants to be her boyfriend,' said Amber, now trying to stop herself from laughing.

'AMBER! You weren't meant to say anything!' said Poppy loudly while nudging her.

I gave them both death glares. Could this be going any worse?

I couldn't bring myself to even look at Daniel. I just stared at his new green-and-white Nike Dunks that he was scuffing into the stones and wished I could disappear under the pebbles.

Daniel Staring at me

Mega awks vibes

me Staring at his Dunks

'Oh, right,' said Theo, sounding confused and looking between me and Daniel, 'but I thought you two were meant to be boyfriend and girl–'

'Well, glad you had a good one,' interrupted Daniel. 'Guess we'll see you around at school. Come on, Theo, or we'll be late.' And then he walked off without even waiting for a reply.

'Right, yeh. See you round,' Theo said to us, following him.

'AMBER! How could you?' I said as soon as they were out of earshot.

'Yeh, that was mean,' agreed Jess. 'It really wasn't any of your business.'

'Oh, come on, guys – lighten up. I was just messing and, anyway, it's best it's out in the open, right?'

'But I asked you not to say anything!' I said.

Amber rolled her eyes and went back to scrolling through Instagram on her phone. Clearly she didn't understand that she'd done anything wrong.

'I mean, maybe she's right and it is best that Daniel knows,' reasoned Molly. 'You did say that you wanted to forget about boys this year, so you could say that Amber has saved you from having a difficult conversation.'

'Yeh. Exactly. I was only being a good friend,' said Amber, smiling sweetly.

I sighed. I was never going to win this battle.

'I have to say though . . .' Amber continued. 'Daniel did look quite hot! Did you see his new Dunks? Très cool if you ask me.'

GRRRRRRR. I am trying so hard to be friends with Amber this year but she's already making it pretty difficult!!

THOUGHT OF THE DAY:
I know what you are thinking. *Lottie
DID say that she wanted to forget about
boys* . . . Well, yes, OK. Maybe I did and
maybe I still do . . . but also maybe I
changed my mind . . .

Feeling very confused right now. Part of
me is mad. Part of me is relieved. Part
of me feels guilty, and part of me is
worrying that maybe I've made a massive
mistake . . . because Amber was right
about one thing - Daniel *did* look pretty
hot in those new Dunks.

WEDNESDAY 31 AUGUST

Went into town with Jess and we spent about two hours in WHSmith choosing stationery – although it was very difficult to steer myself away from the novelty pencil cases, especially the one shaped like a sloth . . .

I managed to refrain! Go me.

I got a turquoise-and-purple leopard-print fluffy pencil case with a pom-pom on the end instead. OK, OK, I know that's not exactly super sophisticated either . . . and come to think about it nor is the red-panda-shaped pencil sharpener . . . but whatevs.

When I got home, I unpacked all my new pens and pencils and put them in the fluffy pencil case and packed them inside my new bag. There is something sooooo satisfying about doing that – it feels like a total fresh start.

Mum also bought me some new school shoes, but I won't talk much about them because they are AWFUL. I used to wear DMs, but now my feet are adult sizes Mum said she can't afford to buy me them any more – sad times.

THURSDAY 1 SEPTEMBER

Waited a couple of days before sending my reply to
Antoine, as I wanted to look like I was busy enjoying life
and not sitting indoors spending way too many hours
composing a 200-word email.

I don't have anyone to help me translate so I wrote back
in English with the odd French word thrown in to make it
look like I'd made an effort. Hugo can always translate it
back to him, I guess – although God knows how badly!

> **From: Lottie Brooks**
> **To: Antoine Roux**
> **Subject: RE: I love cheese**
>
> **Dear Antoine,**
>
> **It was très fantastique to hear from you!**
>
> **It has been nice being back home and seeing
> my friends, but I do miss the 'village of
> tents', all the friends I made there and, of
> course, you.**

To answer your questions:

1. I would rather be a dog, because you get to live in a house and have a nice family to look after you and play catch with you and give you tummy tickles. I would not want to eat those crispy pig ears you can buy in pet shops though – gross!

2. When I grow up, I'd like to be an author or cartoonist because I love to write and draw! In fact here is a little cartoon strip I drew about how we met . . .

3. I absolutely would not choose cheddar, no way – I am much more sophisticated than that! My cheese of choice would either be

Cheestrings or Laughing Cow triangles – yum! BTW have you ever tried Dairylea Lunchables? That is where you get crackers, cheese and ham in a small plastic pot. I enjoy making big stacks and then trying to fit them into my mouth like this . . .

I think this might be a new record!

4. The meaning of life I think is to enjoy yourself and eat as many KitKat Chunkys, Monster Munch and Pot Noodles as possible. ☺

Would you mind if I asked you some questions in return?

1. If you could be a donkey or a hippo, which would you choose?

2. Have you ever tried pickled-onion Monster Munch? It is a sophistiqué et délicieux snack of puffed corn! I have posted some for you to try – enjoy!

3. Would you rather eat a spoonful of your own snot or a spoonful of your own ear wax?

4. What do you think happens to you when you die?

L'amour de, Lottie x

I hope he replies soon!

SATURDAY 3 SEPTEMBER

I can't believe the summer is nearly over – I was hoping to go back to school looking like a bronzed LA goddess, but now I've been back in the UK for a couple of weeks my tan has faded and I look more like a pasty East Sussex . . . What's the opposite of goddess?! I dunno . . . goat?! Yeh. I look like a goat.

WhatsApped the girls:

ME: Just looking in the mirror and realized I look like a goat.

AMBER: I was just thinking the other day that you looked like a goat!

ME: Erm . . . thanks. What can I do about it?

AMBER: Fake tan and highlights!

ME: Are you sure?

AMBER: Do you want to go back to school looking like a goat?

ME: I guess not.

MOLLY: I really wouldn't worry about it, Lottie. Goat stands for 'Greatest Of All Time'!

JESS: Yeh, it's definitely not a baaaaaad thing.

AMBER: Hey, guys – stop butting in!

MOLLY: Sorry, we were just kidding about.

POPPY: Well, I have to admit the whole thing seems a bit eGOATistical.

JESS: I think you are all being silly billies!

ME: V funny, guys 😕

SUNDAY 4 SEPTEMBER

Amber called me. She said she went to Boots and bought some fake tan and a highlighting kit and that I should come round to her house now so that we could put #operationGOAT into practice.

It sounded more like an order than a request. I said I was unsure. She said: 'What can possibly go wrong?'

Probably quite a lot, but I must admit that I do quite like having my own hashtag!

11.34 a.m.

Turns out a lot can go wrong!! We have applied the fake tan and I look like a carrot/goldfish/traffic cone/cheese ball/a very orange thing!

I think Amber went wrong by purchasing a shade called 'Ultra Dark Mahogany Goddess'.

I do not look like a Mahogany Goddess; I look more like an ugly wardrobe.

She said not to worry and that it should fade over the next few days and also look a lot less noticeable when we have done the hair highlights. She showed me the box, and the nice lady on it has really lovely hair, so I'll hopefully look just like her!

12.03 p.m.

I am sitting here with a rubber cap on my head with lots of random hairs pulled through – I now look like some sort of strange alien or sea creature (who is also orange). I can't imagine the nice lady on the box doing this, but I guess she must have done?

12.15 p.m.

The hair is going kind of orangey.

Amber says I need to 'trust the process' and it will go blonde soon.

She must be right because the nice lady on the box has very lovely golden-blonde hair and it's not orange at all.

12.25 p.m.

Still ORANGE! Process, where are you?! I need you!
I NEED TO LOOK LIKE THE NICE LADY ON THE BOX.

12.45 p.m.

Note to self: **NEVER EVER DO HOME HIGHLIGHTS AGAIN**.

The process is not to be trusted. The process is a liar!!

My hair looks nothing like the nice lady on the box!!!

Amber says it will look better when it has been washed and dried . . .

1.02 p.m.

I want to cry. It does not look better once washed and dried. My hair is an orange, stripy mess that looks even worse because of my orange skin.

#OperationGOAT has become #OperationTIGER

Devastated.

What's worse is that Amber has deserted me in my hour of need. She said she had a piano lesson and pushed me out of the front door – I don't even think she has a piano?!

1.56 p.m.

Ran all the way home with my sweatshirt pulled over my head. Couldn't really see where I was going, so I kept bumping into stuff.

Rushed upstairs to the bathroom and gave my face a good scrub, applied a thick layer of foundation, then put on a beanie hat, jeans and a long-sleeved T-shirt.

The plan is foolproof, except that it is 23°C today and you can still see my orange hands.

6.25 p.m.

Stayed in my room all afternoon sweating. Apparently the fake tan should wear off in the next week or so, but I will have to wait until my orange hair grows out before I can go out in public. I've googled it and hair grows about 1.25 centimetres every month so that should only take about one and a half years. Perfectly doable.

Oh God – Dad's just called upstairs and dinner's ready. I hadn't factored in how I was going to deal with family mealtimes . . . I guess I could maybe ask for my dinner to be delivered to my room on a tray. Perhaps Dad could cut a hatch into my door, but not sure Mum will go for that?!

I put on sunglasses and gloves and tried to act as casual as possible, but they immediately became suspicious.

I had no choice but to come clean and after everyone had stopped laughing – no joke, it was about ten minutes of solid LOLs – Mum was actually quite cross with me. She said she'd have never let me dye my own hair if she'd known about it. It should be left to the professionals and anyway I'm far too young.

Dad scoffed and said, 'You've had hair every colour of the rainbow since I met you, Laura. Remember when you accidentally dyed it green?'

She said, 'Yes . . . well . . . I guess we all make mistakes.'

The good news is that she is taking me to the hairdresser's tomorrow to get it sorted – the bad news is that it's coming out of my pocket money.

MONDAY 5 SEPTEMBER

The hair is fixed! The hairdresser is a miracle worker and I LOVE MY MUM SO MUCH, because she let me get some subtle highlights and they are just the best.

She also made a magic potion using some baking soda, lemon and baby oil that she mixed up, and then I rubbed it all over my body using an exfoliation mitt and it's removed pretty much all the horrible orange tan.

So I'm not exactly looking like a bronzed LA goddess, but I'm not exactly a pasty goat/orange tiger either. I'm somewhere in between the two . . . A funky chipmunk perhaps?!

When I went to show off the new me to the boys, Toby said I looked like a 'poo head' and Dad said I looked exactly the same as I did before.

Mum said, 'Honestly, you spend a hundred pounds getting your hair done and that's the verdict!'

Dad said, 'HOW MUCH?!?'

Mum said, 'That's what it costs and she's paying it back out of her own money!'

Dad said, 'My haircuts used to cost six quid!'

Mum said, 'Oh, here we go again . . . You've not had any hair for over ten years, Bill.'

Dad said, 'Kick a man when he's down . . . It's not my fault I'm lacking in the follicular department. And anyway I thought you said you liked my bald head.'

Mum went over to him and put her arms around him. 'I do . . . I find it VERY attractive.'

Dad said, 'Oh, really . . .' And they started smooching again.

I said, 'Please, guys – can't you just be normal? This sort of behaviour is highly damaging to a pre-teen.' Then I quickly exited the room.

THOUGHT OF THE DAY:
I really hope Mum isn't seriously expecting me to pay her for my hair out of my already meagre weekly pocket money!!

TUESDAY 6 SEPTEMBER

I can't believe this is the last day of the holidays! It feels like the summer's gone really quickly but at the same time it feels like it's been ages since we've been at school.

I'm kind of looking forward to going back but . . . life is so simple in the holidays.

Sometimes I look at my hammies and I think, *Wow, those guys have a pretty great life.* No school, no work, no chores, no worrying about what to wear.

I mean, it would certainly be easier if humans were covered in fur and we didn't have to wear clothes, wouldn't it? We could just go on our wheels, stuff our little faces full of food, and then sleep.

Pretty perfect if you ask me. I guess the downside is that hammies only live for about two to three years, but at least they don't have to worry about mortgages and pensions.

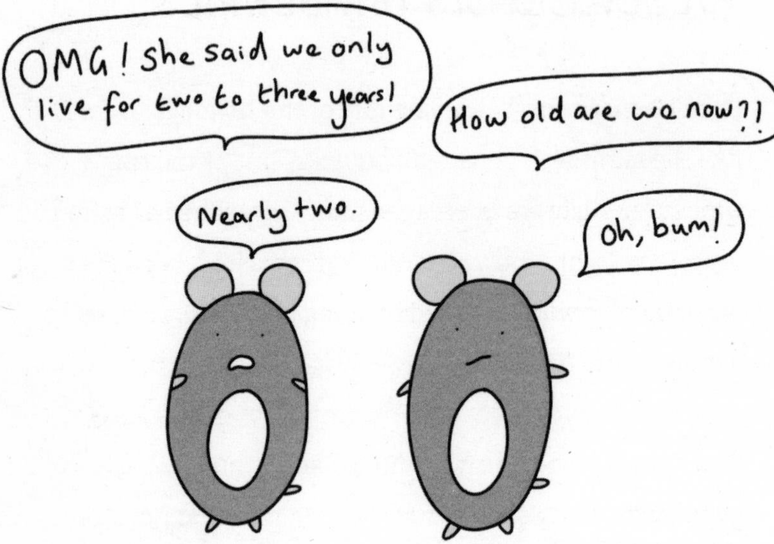
OMG! She said we only live for two to three years!
How old are we now?!
Nearly two.
Oh, bum!

WEDNESDAY 7 SEPTEMBER

6.35 a.m.

Up ridiculously early because today is my first day
as a Year Eight – wow! I'm a little bit excited, because
although we will have boring lessons (YAWN) at least I
get to see my friends all day every day again. Plus, we
won't be the youngest in the school any more – WAHOO!

4.57 p.m.

It was so funny seeing all the new Year Sevens this
morning – they looked so small and scared. I can't
believe a year ago that was me. It feels like FOREVER ago.

I think me and my friends all enjoyed feeling mature and
experienced. I tried to give the Year Sevens reassuring
smiles though . . . and a few smug looks too (soz –
couldn't help it) . . . Oh, and I may have accidentally on
purpose sent a group of three of them in completely the
wrong direction when they were looking for the art room,
but it was only a bit of harmless fun.

We have Mr Peters for our form tutor again this year because we keep the same form tutors all the way through at Kingswood High. I'm really glad about that – Mr Peters is super nice and kind and only strict when he needs to be.

Anyway . . . LOADS happened today so I best get on and tell you all about it or we will be here all night, won't we?

SO here we go:

1. We have a new girl in our class. She's called Isha, which she said is Hindi for 'one who protects' – how nice is that? She told us that her grandparents moved to the UK from India when her mum was ten and that her family have just moved to Brighton from Croydon because her dad has a new job as a doctor at Royal Sussex Hospital. Isha is super smiley and friendly, so when Mr Peters asked who would like to be Isha's official buddy for the week we all put our hands up. He picked Jess, which was good, as it means I'll get to hang out with Isha lots too.

Isha

2. We are going away over half-term on a residential. I mean, we knew about this last year because our parents had to pay the deposits and stuff like that, but that was ages ago and – since I'd been so busy with my MEGA-COMPLICATED love life and worrying about looking like a goat – I'd almost forgotten all about it. Today Mr Peters talked about the trip and that made it seem a lot more real.

We're going to a place called Camp Firefly and we'll be doing loads of different types of activities like raft building (fun), abseiling (scary) and drama (fun and scary). We'll be away from Monday to Friday and it's the longest I've ever been away from my family. A lot of kids did residential trips in their primary schools, but my school was really small, so apart from sleepovers at friends' houses I've never been away from my parents AT ALL. I'm half super excited and half super nervous about it.

I think I'll miss Mum (quite a lot), Dad (a little bit), Bella (a tiny bit) and Toby (not at all). In fact, one of the biggest bonuses of the trip is being totally Toby-free and more importantly I won't be smelling his tasty air biscuits for nearly a week! My nostrils will be in heaven! Wahoo!

3. Mr Peters handed out our new timetables and, as soon as tutor time finished, the TQOEG and Isha gathered in the corridor outside to compare them. Mine massively sucks because I used to have nearly ALL my lessons with Jess and now we are in different classes for about half of them. We're together in maths though, which I'm super relieved about, because let's just say that maths isn't my strongest skill and Jess has to help me out when I get stuck.

The rest of the day was OK. We didn't do too much work in the lessons; it was mostly teachers talking about what we were going to be learning and then handing out new exercise books. At lunch we gave Isha a tour of the school and pointed out all the super-important stuff like the haunted janitor cupboard, which toilet cubicles had broken locks, and which dinner ladies gave the biggest portions of chips.

And some of the less important stuff . . . like why I have so many stupid nicknames . . .

Then we all got cheese paninis for lunch and made our way over to our favourite table in the canteen. It felt great being back with the gang again and good to welcome Isha too.

'So, what sort of stuff are you into?' Poppy asked her.

'Oh, loads of stuff, but mostly at the minute I'm into football. I can do one hundred and forty-seven keepy-uppies . . .'

'OMG,' shrieked Jess. 'That's amazing! I love football too,

but I can only do a hundred and twenty-five.'

Isha grinned. 'Cool! I'd love to play for the school – do you know if they have a team?'

'They have a boys' team . . . but I don't think they have a girls' team,' said Poppy.

'Well, that's majorly sexist!' said Isha.

'You are SO right,' said Jess. 'Maybe we could get a team together. Let's talk to Mr Lewis about it – he's our PE teacher.'

Isha high-fived her. 'Great idea!'

I smiled, but I felt a little strange inside hearing Jess and Isha talking so excitedly; it seems like they have a lot in common.

'What do you think about living in Brighton so far?' I asked Isha, keen to get involved in the conversation.

'I love it – it's great being by the sea. The seagulls are a bit annoying though. They woke me up at three o'clock last night with their squawking, and on Saturday one swooped at me while I was eating chips on the beach and knocked them out of my hand!'

'Ha, you'll get used to it,' replied Poppy.

'Yep, you just have to keep your wits about you,' agreed Molly.

'One time, this HUGE, mean-looking seagull dive-bombed my burger outside H&M,' said Amber, looking properly annoyed about it.

'That was, like, two years ago!' groaned Poppy.

'SO?! It was a Big Mac, and I hadn't even taken a bite!!'

We all laughed – trust Amber to still hold a grudge against a seagull.

When I got home, M&D were really eager to hear about how I got on, so I filled them in over spaghetti and meatballs. I told them all about Isha and the trip – how

I was excited but also worried I might be a bit homesick being away for that long.

'Lottie, if you are really worried, I could always call the school and volunteer as a parent helper?' said Dad.

I replied as politely as I could . . .

I hope that was clear.

THURSDAY 8 SEPTEMBER

I know EXACTLY what you are wondering – what's going on with Daniel, huh? Why didn't Lottie mention him yesterday?!

Well, the answer is that I purposely didn't mention him because I am trying not to think about him, and I didn't want you to think that I was thinking about him either . . . which is stupid really because you are just my private diary and incapable of making judgements about me . . .

OR ARE YOU?!?!

Sometimes I get this funny feeling that maybe other people are reading these crazy ramblings of mine and know all sorts about my life . . . Do you think that could actually happen?! I mean, imagine if someone found this diary and sent it off to a publisher and they printed it and put it into bookshops for thousands of random kids to read?!?! I'd be absolutely mortified!

OH, SHUT UP, LOTTIE – THAT WOULD BE INSANE!

So now we've cleared that up, let's go back to being honest . . .

I didn't mention Daniel yesterday because I guess I'm trying to put him to the back of my mind. Plus, as we are in different forms and our school is quite big, I only saw him from a distance.

I was wondering if we'd share any classes together at all, but today when I walked into science with Molly, he was sitting next to Theo at the back and my heart started beating really fast.

'What's wrong, Lottie? You've gone really pale,' said Molly, clearly clocking my increasing awkwardness.

'Oh, nothing,' I whispered. 'Just that I'm about to come face to face with my ex-boyfriend who doesn't like me because he thinks I met an HFB and forgot all about him.'

'Well, you did, didn't you?'

'Only temporarily . . .'

'So, you like him again now?' asked Molly.

'I don't know . . . I guess it would just be nice if we could be friends, y'know?'

'Well, if you want to be friends with him, then maybe you should try talking to him . . .'

But that's easier said than done when you're someone like me who seems to babble nonsense whenever I am nervous.

Anyway, it turned out that we didn't even make eye contact, and when the lesson was over he was out of the door before I'd even finished packing up my stuff.

I was kind of relieved but also a little sad. I guess what I mean is that I'd really like things to be OK between us, but I'm worried that, after what Amber said the other day, he's cross with me.

After school, me and Jess walked home with Isha. They were talking about which football teams they support: Isha supports Arsenal, but now she lives down here she'd like to start supporting Brighton too, like Jess. They said they'd like to go to a game together some time. They invited me too and I said it sounded fun, even though I think football is one of the dullest things to ever exist.

I guess I didn't really like the thought of them doing something together without me, which I know is kind of silly because, even if Jess does have other friends, we'll always be BFFs.

SATURDAY 10 SEPTEMBER

OOH! Antoine has replied!

> From: Antoine Roux
> To: Lottie Brooks
> Subject: RE: RE: I love cheese
>
> Bonjour Lottie,
>
> It is such a super feeling in my liver to hear from yourself.
>
> Firstly, let me break some unsettling news – it has not been a happy time in the world of Antoine. Since we last had internet connections, I have contracted a horrible illness called Gigantic Thumb Disease. It is where my thumbs suddenly grow to be five times as big as is usual for a thumb.
>
> A bit like this . . .

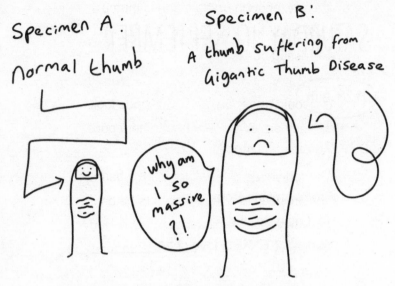

I feel sad to see myself in the mirror with strange massive thumbs but, as ma mère says, 'Nobody is perfect!' and she so correctly see it! Antoine is not defined by his thumbs!

My question to you, Lottie. Will you still consider me a boyfriend even despite my illness?

If you prefer a normal-size thumb, I would not blame you. I would simply make a life-size papier-mâché model of you and throw it into a bonfire.

Anyway, enough of the gigantic thumb chitty-chat! Let me answer your super-interesting questions!

1. I would rather be donkey. Hippos look like they are doing very bad bottom pops.

2. I tried your pickled-onion maize-based monstrosities and found them to be an insult to my tastebuds. You seem to have many disgusting foods in England – what a puzzle of the mind.

3. I enjoy eating both earwax and snot equally, but if I must choose a spoonful of one: snot.

4. When we die, good people become unicorns and bad people become microwaves. Not much else happens.

Tell me about your school? Is it pointless? Do you have friendships? Is there a toilet?

Much of my love,

Antoine x

Despite its sad content, the email made me laugh so much. I was sorry to hear about Antoine's thumbs, but his mum is right: no one is perfect.

The most concerning part of the email was that he hated Monster Munch. I mean, who hates Monster Munch?! That's just insanity!!

11.45 a.m.

I looked up Gigantic Thumb Disease on the NHS website and couldn't find any mention of it. Perhaps it's so super rare that Antoine is the only case?

It's hard to know if dating someone with really large thumbs would be a problem for me. I would like to think not, but I guess it's difficult to say without seeing them in person.

3.55 p.m.

Mum and Dad took us out for lunch as a back-to-school treat.

I'm not sure why they thought going out for lunch would be a fun thing to do because TBH it NEVER ends well. I mean, I'm not the problem. I probably have the best table manners out of the lot of them – but they keep forgetting they have an eight-month-old baby (who is more like an angry monkey) and an eight-year-old son (who is more like a . . . a . . . I don't even know how to describe Toby – he's almost beyond words).

So, we went to our local pub, the King's Head, because that's Dad's 'favourite place in the world' even though it was meant to be a treat for me and Toby – go figure!

Anyway, the problems started when I tried to order from the adult menu and Dad was all like: 'Lottie, the kids' menu is £6.99 and includes a drink AND ice cream, whereas an adult pizza is £14 on its own.'

'So?'

'So it's much better value!'

'Because it's like half the size, Dad!'

I mean, the menu is for twelves and under, and I'm nearly thirteen FGS – so it's hardly applicable to me, and the portions are tiny. And by 'tiny', I mean 'MINISCULE'! Barely even enough to feed a flea . . .

When the food arrived, I was proved right because my pizza was so small you needed a microscope to see it. Then Toby started kicking off because he'd ordered sausage and chips, but because there were peas on the plate that had touched the chips he refused to eat them, and because the sausages had a 'weird herby taste' he refused to eat those either.

Meanwhile Bella screamed pretty much the entire way through the meal. Mum put her in a high chair and tried to feed her some sort of jarred pasta baby food and she was fuming. She kept wanting to eat our chips instead and Mum said chips are not a recommended food for weaning babies.

After the waitress had cleared the main dishes away, she brought me and Toby our kiddy pudding, which was ice cream in a bowl with wafers and jelly beans on top.

I said, 'I'm not eating that! It looks like it's for a five-year-old.'

Dad reached across the table to take it. 'Well, don't worry – I'll eat it then.'

I grabbed it quickly away from him. He should know that I'm only being annoying on purpose. Then I ate it while hiding behind a menu.

Bella was still screaming the place down, and by that time Mum had lost the will to live so she just handed Toby's leftover chips to Bella. But that wasn't enough – because she wanted Mum's wine too!

'There's no way you are having wine at eight months old, Bella Brooks!' Mum said crossly.

Bella wailed and started flailing her arms in anger so much so that she knocked Mum's glass out of her hand, and it went flying across the room and smashed into a million pieces. You should have seen the looks we were getting from the other tables!

Mum was upset because she hadn't even taken a sip of the wine yet, Dad was upset because it cost £8.50 a glass, I was upset about my doll's-house-sized dinner, Toby was upset about the pea contamination, and Bella was upset because she was too young for proper chairs/chips/wine. In short, it was a total disaster, so we all ate up quickly and got out of there as fast as we could.

On the way home, Dad said, 'Well, that was a massive waste of fifty quid!'

He says that every time, but he'll have forgotten about it in a month and we'll be back again trying to enjoy a 'nice family meal'. I don't know why he keeps trying – it's really NOT POSSIBLE.

Maybe next time he wants to treat me and Toby, he should just give us £25 each and be done with it.

Called Jess for advice about my Antoine predicament . . .

'If you liked someone . . .' I asked her, 'would it put you off them if you found out they had really massive thumbs?'

'Have you had one too many KitKat Chunkys this morning, Lottie?'

'No . . . I'm just curious . . .'

'Well, it depends how much bigger.'

'About five times as big.'

'Well, it might be a bit strange – like, how would you hold hands?'

'Hmm . . . dunno . . .'

'But ultimately it doesn't matter – it's what's on the inside that counts. Plus, imagine how good they would be at thumb wars!'

'Jess, you are SO wise.'

'I know . . . Now do you have any other hugely important questions or can I get back to doing the Biscuit Face Challenge.'

'What's the Biscuit Face Challenge?'

'It's where you have to get a biscuit from your forehead into your mouth using only your facial movements.'

'Ah, well, sorry to interrupt such important business, but I have just one more question . . . When you die, would you rather be a unicorn or a microwave?'

'Lottie Brooks, you are seriously weird.'

'Takes a weirdo to know a weirdo!'

'True dat.'

THOUGHT OF THE DAY:
I personally think ninety-nine per cent of people would rather be a unicorn, so I think I'd rather be a microwave as I like to be different!

SUNDAY 11 SEPTEMBER

Jess came round and we spent about two hours trying to do the Biscuit Face Challenge.

It's a lot harder than it looks but very funny. I kept getting mine stuck in my eye socket and I think Jess was getting a bit distracted and just eating them, tsk tsk.

Even my family couldn't resist having a go. Dad is the only one who has managed to do it, but I think he has an unfair advantage because of his beard – it gives extra grip.

It seems that certain biscuits are better than others too: round ones are definitely a good idea, and if you are using a chocolate one, make sure the chocolate is facing up to avoid meltage.

7.18 p.m.

I've been thinking about Antoine's email a lot and debating whether accepting his girlfriend invitation would be a good idea.

Pros of going out with Antoine:

* He's hot.

* We have a few things in common (like cheese and, errr . . . actually, I think that's it).

* Won't have to share my Monster Munch with him.

* Can tell everyone I have a French boyfriend, which makes me sound très sophisticated!

Cons of going out with Antoine:

* Language barrier.

* Lives far away.

* Unlikely to ever see him again.

* Potential thumb weirdness.

* He's not Daniel. ☹

It's a really tough one – and even the hamsters can't agree!

I know that me and Daniel aren't a thing any more, but I still get all nervous when I see him – does that mean I like him?! He's been looking especially cute lately . . .

I think I'll have to see what happens when I see him next week and whether there is any 'romantic spark' left between us at all.

MONDAY 12 SEPTEMBER

I was telling the girls at lunch about the Daniel vs Antoine situ and how it felt almost impossible to know which one was the right one for me.

Poppy suggested making a paper fortune teller. It was as good an idea as any, so I said why not.

She then spent about twenty minutes making it, before proudly declaring: 'It's done!'

'OK,' said Poppy. 'Lottie, ask the fortune teller anything!'

'Cool – my first question is . . . should I say yes to being Antoine's girlfriend?'

'Great – now pick a colour.'

'GREEN.'

Poppy started spelling it out: **'G-R-E-E-N** . . . Now pick a number.'

'SEVEN.'

She counted to seven and then said, 'Pick another number.'

'ONE!'

She lifted up the flap to read my fortune. 'Hmm . . . you will get eaten alive by a gang of angry crows.'

'WHAT?!'

'OK. Sorry, yeh . . . Maybe that one was a bit strange – let's try again.'

We went through the process again and this time I picked seven as my last number. Poppy lifted up the flap. 'OOH, this one's good – you will find £5 in the street and spend it on a frozen lasagne!'

'Poppy – I thought this was meant to be a fortune teller to help me make a decision between Antoine and Daniel. How are any of these things relevant? Also, if I found £5 in the street, why would I choose to spend it on a frozen lasagne?!'

I grabbed the fortune teller off her and opened up the rest of it. This is what it said . . .

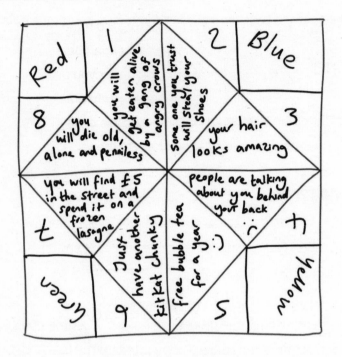

I looked at her with my mouth hanging open. What was she thinking?!

'Mmmm, sorry,' she said. 'Perhaps I got a bit distracted. Maybe you should just flip a coin instead?'

'Fine.' I found a 10p in my wallet. 'Heads for Daniel, tails for Antoine.'

I flipped it, and we all watched as it flew through the air and rolled under the table. I ducked under the table to find the coin.

'Tails,' I said, sighing. 'I guess it's Antoine then.'

'You sound disappointed,' said Molly.

'I think I am, but if the coin has decided, then that's that – it's over with Daniel for good.'

'Lottie, that's ridiculous!' said Amber.

'Yeh, the coin doesn't really get to decide,' agreed Molly. 'If the coin comes up with a result and you're disappointed with it, then that means you should do the opposite of what it says.'

I look at her. 'Really?!'

'Yes, silly,' said Molly. 'The coin isn't the law. It's only there to help you admit your real feelings.'

I clapped my hands together. 'It did! It helped me realize who I wanted – it's Daniel!'

So that was that. The decision had been made. Now I just have to hope against hope that he feels the same way.

PS Something very strange and unsettling happened on the way home from school. Firstly, I found a £5 note on the pavement outside Sainsbury's. Before I knew what I was doing, I had walked through the doors and was standing in the frozen-food section taking a lasagne out of the freezer.

Then as I was walking home, carrier bag in hand, I heard a chilling squawk behind me. I spun round to see five large black crows. They started to fly towards me, and I wasn't going to hang around to see if they wanted me for their dinner – me and my lasagne RAN as fast as we could!

When I got home, I was out of breath and terrified.

Mum said, 'Oh gosh, Lottie, what's wrong?'

I couldn't speak so I just handed her the Sainsbury's bag. She was so delighted with the lasagne and the fact that she wouldn't have to cook dinner that she forgot all about my welfare and walked off to preheat the oven.

I crawled upstairs to my room and got under the duvet; it was only then that I realized how close to death I'd been. When my hands had stopped shaking, I texted Poppy.

> **ME:** DESTROY THE FORTUNE TELLER BEFORE SOMEONE GETS HURT!!
> 🍴 🐦 💀

TUESDAY 13 SEPTEMBER

According to Molly, when you've fallen out with someone and want to make up, you should 'offer them an olive branch'.

There are a few problems with that:

1. I don't have an olive tree or an olive branch.

2. Our next-door neighbours have an olive tree, but I suspect they may be a bit annoyed if I went into their garden and hacked a branch off it.

3. Why would anyone want an olive branch anyway?! It's a stupid saying that makes zero sense.

4. Or I guess the olive branch may have olives on it, so the point is . . . a gift of olives?

5.) I actually think olives are GROSS so it
wouldn't work for me.

I explained all this to Molly, and she said, 'It's
metaphorical, silly.'

WHAT?!

'I think you are confusing me with someone who understands big words,' I replied.

'I mean, it's meant to be a peace offering. You can swap the olive branch for whatever you like . . . Maybe give him your crisps or something?'

My heart sank. I had pickled-onion Monster Munch for lunch today and I'd been really looking forward to them.

'I think I'd rather go back to the olive branch,' I said sadly.

'Calm down – you don't have to give him the whole bag! Just offer him one maybe?'

'You only get about seven Monster Munch in a packet!'

'Well, you have to decide whether he's worth it, Lottie . . .'

It was a VERY difficult decision. I HATE sharing Monster Munch. TBH I think everyone hates sharing Monster Munch . . . If someone offers you a Frazzle and expects a Monster Munch back in return, it's just not a fair trade.

The QUEEN of crisps

HRH

Also good but completely UNFAIR trades

I never win anything :(

But I'm getting distracted . . . Molly was right – I had to be the bigger person here. And I did like Daniel more than Monster Munch (possibly).

I got the opportunity at break time. It was nice and sunny, and I was sitting on the playing field with Poppy when Molly and Amber came over with Daniel and Theo. They sat down next to us, and Molly raised her eyebrows and nudged me as if to say, *Do it now*.

I took the Monster Munch packet out of my bag, slowly opened it and looked longingly inside at the sour nuggets of deliciousness. He'd better appreciate this grand gesture!

'Want one, Daniel?' I said, offering him the bag.

'Nah,' he replied without even making eye contact. 'They make your breath stink.'

I was SHOOK!

And then to top it off he opened his Wotsits and ate them all without offering me one, even though you get about twenty of those in a packet!

I obviously mean very little to him if I'm not even worth one lousy cheese puff. ☹

THOUGHT OF THE DAY:
I would like to officially retract my statement that I like Daniel more than Monster Munch. I'm sorry, Monster Munch, it was very foolish of me.

WEDNESDAY 14 SEPTEMBER

The girls have all agreed that the romance is definitely over – the light has gone out, the spark is nowhere to be seen, the torch has run out of batteries, the electrics have short-circuited, the bulb has blown. It is over with Daniel FOR GOOD!

So I am free to see whomever I choose, and I may as well choose Antoine . . . even though he lives in a different country so it's kinda pointless – but whatevs. I'd much rather have an absent boyfriend with Gigantic Thumb Disease than a rude, cheesy-fingered WOTSIT HOGGER!

Wrote back to Antoine to tell him the good news . . .

From: Lottie Brooks
To: Antoine Roux
Subject: RE: RE: RE: I love cheese

Dearest Antoine,

Firstly, I am so sorry to hear that you have contracted Gigantic Thumb Disease. It sounds very distressing. How did you catch it and is there a cure?

Don't worry though – I am not a shallow person, and it does not bother me. In fact, I have been thinking about your proposal and I have decided that, yes, I would like to be your girlfriend! I hope you are happy to hear that.

I apologize it has taken me a while to decide. To be truly honest, the reason is that before we met I had a boyfriend called Daniel and I was unsure about where that relationship was going. Anyway, it turns out that he won't share his crisps, so obviously it's over now.

In other news, school is OK, but – as you say – quite pointless. There are toilets there though, which is useful for . . . well, you know what.

I have four friends called Jess, Amber, Molly and Poppy. We are in a gang called TQOEG, which stands for 'The Queens of Eight Green', and we are all going away on a school trip for five days over half-term, which should be fun! Do you have a gang?

Tell me some things about your life at school and your friends.

Lottie x

PS It's a shame you don't like Monster Munch but I will try not to hold it against you.

THURSDAY 15 SEPTEMBER

I've hardly seen Jess this week. Even in the lessons that we do have together, the new seating plans mean that I'm sat nowhere near her. This is really bad news in maths. Like I told you, I find it really hard and Jess usually helps with explaining stuff to me. I feel too embarrassed to put my hand up and ask for extra help because then everyone will think I'm stupid.

My new timetable really sucks, and a lot of my lessons just before break time and lunch aren't with any of my friends. That means that I'm often wandering around trying to find them.

Today I went into the canteen at lunch and walked over to Molly, Amber and Poppy, who were already sitting down eating.

'Where's Jess?' I said, pulling out a chair.

'She's over there with Isha and TSACG,' Molly replied, pointing.

I looked over to where she was pointing and saw them laughing together.

'What does TSACG mean?' I asked.

'Oh, it's a gang,' said Amber. 'It stands for "The Sporty and Clever Girls".'

'Well, that's a bit arrogant!' I huffed.

'Hmmm . . .' said Molly. 'Maybe, but I guess the Queens of Eight Green sounds a bit arrogant too.'

OK, she wasn't wrong, not that I wanted to admit it.

Amber prodded me and pointed at Isha . . .

I felt a stab of jealousy in my stomach. I mean, why was Jess sitting over there with them? We've sat together at lunch since the first day in Year Seven.

Later on, after school, I went to find Jess so that we could walk home together. I missed her and I was looking forward to chatting, just the two of us.

My heart sank when I saw her coming out of the doors with Isha. They were deep in conversation about something that had happened in their art class. I walked over to join them.

'OMG, did you see when Leo flicked a massive blob of purple paint in Nate's hair?' said Isha.

'I know, it was hilarious – he's so funny!' replied Jess.

I tried to laugh along with them, but it's hard to get involved when you weren't actually there.

WhatsApp convo with Jess:

ME: Hey, BFF, I've missed you this week – where have you been?

JESS: I know, I'm sorry – I've missed you too! Me and Isha and a few others have been hatching a plan to get Mr Lewis to agree to the school having a girls' football team.

ME: Oh, cool. How's it going?

JESS: Good. I mean I think he's unsure about the extra work involved but if enough girls want to do it, then he can't really say no as that would be pretty sexist, don't you think?

ME: For sure. How are you doing with the Biscuit Face Challenge? I got a custard cream past my nose yesterday!

JESS: Whoop! That's amazing – I got a Rich Tea to the corner of my mouth and then it fell off. Gutted!

ME: We'll get there.

JESS: We will 😔

I feel a bit better for messaging her. I know that she is doing a good thing and that I should try really hard not to feel envious of her and Isha's friendship.

FRIDAY 16 SEPTEMBER

Great day today! Not.

The day itself was OK, as school days go, but after our last lesson I had that Friday feeling in my toes and I wanted to do something to celebrate, so after the final bell I said to the girls: 'Who fancies getting some chips from Frydays to toast the end of our first full week as Year Eights?'

'Sorry, Lottie, I can't – it's my dad's birthday,' said Poppy.

'Yeh, we can't either. Molly is coming over to mine,' said Amber, linking arms with Molly and dragging her off.

I turned to Jess. 'Oh well. Looks like it's just you and me.'

She shifted about awkwardly from one foot to the other. 'Well, actually, Lottie . . . Isha's invited me round to her house today . . . so . . .'

She gave a little wave and walked off to find Isha, and

then I was left standing on the kerb outside school by myself watching everyone else head to Frydays with their mates.

I felt like a right Lonely Lottie No Mates. ☹

Then, to make it worse, I had to walk past Frydays and I saw Isha and Jess in there getting chips with TSACG! I'm getting a bit worried that she keeps hanging out with them TBH.

I couldn't bear to go in after that, so I went to the newsagent's and bought myself a can of Rio and a KitKat Chunky to cheer myself up. Only it didn't work. It really hurt being left out like that. Particularly by Jess.

When I got home, I walked into the kitchen, and Toby and another little boy I'd not seen before were sat eating Rice Krispie cakes at the table.

'This is my new friend, Oscar,' announced Toby. 'Oscar, this is my sister Lottie. She's an idiot and she smells.'

Happy Friday, everybody, from Lottie, AKA the friendless, smelly idiot!

SATURDAY 17 SEPTEMBER

I am feeling a bit strange today. Everything seems like it is changing . . .

* I hate my new timetable.

* No one has any time for me.

* Jess and Isha are probably going to become BFFs.

* I have stupid eyebrows.

* My feet aren't in proportion to the rest of me (size six already).

* In short – what is the point of me?

I feel really rejected, so I can't even bear to message my friends to see if anyone wants to meet up in case they all have plans and then I'll feel **EVEN MORE** of a loser.

God, what if they're doing something together and I'm not invited?! That would be the worst.

10.55 a.m.

As if I'm not aware of all my own faults, Toby just poked this drawing under my door! ☹

I was watching TV in bed and Mum came and knocked on the door.

'Do you want to come to town with me, Lottie? I'm popping to Churchill Square to get some new underwear.'

I sighed. 'No offence, Mum, but the shopping centre is full of school kids on a Saturday, and I don't want to be seen with you in public . . . especially when you're shopping for underwear!'

She laughed. 'None taken – we could always split up for a bit?'

'That would be even worse!' I tell her. 'No one goes into town on their own. It looks like you've got no friends!'

'Well, why don't you message Jess or Molly and see if they want to meet you?'

'Because I'm busy watching –' I glanced up at the TV – '*Gardeners' World*.'

'Since when do you like *Gardeners' World*?'

'It's a good episode – they're building a pergola and discussing the pros and cons of ornamental water features.'

'Oh, come on, Lottie. This is silly. What's wrong?'

I reluctantly showed her the list I'd written, and I was glad I did because she explained that I have nice eyebrows and that I'm only twelve and have plenty of time to grow into my feet. She also said that it's natural to feel jealous sometimes, but that jealousy is a green-eyed monster and, instead of worrying about Jess and Isha becoming better friends, I should try to find some common ground with them both, so that I can join in and not feel left out.

I said, 'Mum, you are so wise – like a wise, old owl!'

'Thanks, Lottie – but less of the "old" please. I'm only in my early forties.'

I think she's deluding herself personally. Forty is ancient.

Anyway, I hope she's right and that I can find some stuff in common, so I can be friends with Isha too.

(12.20 p.m.)

OOH, a parcel arrived for me from Antoine! It contained a packet of yummy-looking bacon Bugles. I'm excited to try them, but I decided to take them into school and ~~flaunt them around~~ share them with my friends.

THOUGHT OF THE DAY 1:
If jealousy is a green-eyed monster, I wonder what he/she looks like? Maybe the Grinch, Shrek or Mike Wazowski from *Monsters Inc.*?

THOUGHT OF THE DAY 2:
Maybe even though me and Antoine are separated by the Atlantic Ocean we can still have a very happy relationship just posting crisps to each other - pretty perfect if you ask me!

SUNDAY 18 SEPTEMBER

6 a.m.

Had a v v weird dream that I was visited by a green-eyed monster that actually looked more like a strange cabbage with wings! She introduced herself as Angela and kept trying to whisper things into my brain that I didn't want to hear. I hope she doesn't come back again as I didn't like her very much!

Things are on the up today – Antoine has replied!

From: Antoine Roux

To: Lottie Brooks

Subject: RE: RE: RE: RE: I love cheese

Dearest Lottie,

I am so glad to hear you want to be one of
Antoine's girlfriends. That is fantastical
news!

This Daniel geezer sounds like a brown toilet
deposit – who is not wanting to share crispy
items with one of the most beautiful girl that I
have ever seen dropping cutlery?

Anyway, Daniel's stupidness is to Antoine's
beneficials.

Do not worry it was taking you a long
time to come to a decision. I have many
girlfriends and it is always hard to decide

which ones to choose yes and which ones to put into the bin. Antoine is being a very popular guy and I cannot deny my excellent handsomeness.

I am glad to hear you have friends. I also have friends – we are in a gang called Obsessed with Dogs Club. I hope that translates to English. We like to walk about and find nice dogs and give them a pat. Dogs make me happy on my face.

I really enjoy our correspondence. Write back immediately.

Antoine x

PS I hope you receive the bacon Bugles as a declaration of my love for my newest girlfriend and for the proof that I am not a Crisp Scrooge!

PPS You catch Gigantic Thumb Disease by falling into a deep stagnant pond. The cure is to lick the feet of a horse 150 times. It is

quite dangerous, but I have done it
25 times and now my thumb is only three
times normal size.

PPPS Have a fun time on your school trip.
Last time I went on a school trip I was
attacked by an ostrich and nearly died.

Not quite sure how I feel about his email . . . What does
he mean by 'one of Antoine's girlfriends' and 'newest
girlfriend'? I kind of assumed that I would be the only
one, but this sounds a bit like he's talking in the plural
maybe?!

Anyway, let's not worry about the details. The most
important thing is that I have a Hot French BOYFRIEND!!

(3.55 p.m.)

Just back from Jess's house. She called and asked if I
wanted to go round to hers. I can't lie – I was super
relieved.

It was sunny, so we hung out in the garden and practised
front flips on the trampo. Her little sister Florence came

out to bounce with us too. She is so super cute – I can't wait until Bella is a bit older and able to talk and play like Flo.

After we'd been flipping for about an hour, we were tired out, so Jess grabbed a couple of Capri-Suns from the kitchen and we lay down on the trampoline, looking at the clouds. I really wanted to ask her about what happened on Friday when I saw her in the chip shop, but I didn't know how.

There was no other option than to blurt it out, so I took a deep breath. 'You know on Friday when I asked if you wanted to get chips but you said –'

'I know what you are going to say, Lottie, and I'm so sorry! I thought we were going straight back to Isha's house – I didn't know we'd end up in Frydays.'

'That's OK. I guess I just felt a bit left out.'

'You know I would have asked you too, if I had known?'

I breathed a sigh of relief. 'I know.'

'Listen, we'll all get chips next week, yeh? Isha's really great – we should all hang out together more.'

'I'd like that . . . Anyway, I have some news! I think I have a new boyfriend!'

'What do you mean, *you think*?!'

'Well, it was a bit confusing . . .'

I showed Antoine's email to Jess on my phone. After she'd finished laughing, she said that she thought it was probably badly translated but maybe I should check the relationship Ts and Cs with him if I was worried. Hmmmm.

4.43 p.m.

I decided that Jess was right and emailed Antoine back . . .

From: Lottie Brooks
To: Antoine Roux
Subject: RE: RE: RE: RE: RE: I love cheese

Quick question. When you say 'one of my girlfriends', do you mean you have more than one girlfriend?

PS Thank you for the crisps. They look très délicieux!

PPS Glad to hear the thumbs are improving. 👍

PPPS I think your OWD Club sounds awesome! I LOVE dogs too. I might try and start up a club like that in Brighton.

PPPPS What exactly did the ostrich do?!

MONDAY 19 SEPTEMBER

I hadn't heard back from Antoine, so I decided to assume
that his use of plurals was just a translation thing, like
Jess said. I absolutely didn't want to delay announcing
my exciting news, so I went to school armed with the
bacon Bugles, ready to humblebrag.

I made sure to announce VERY loudly that they were
from my Hot French Boyfriend. Everyone was dead
impressed. Hopefully the whole of Year Eight will know
about it by tomorrow. Then Daniel will be sorry for not
sharing his Wotsits with me!

OMG!!!!!!!

LIVID!!!!!!!!!!!!!!!!!!!!!!!!

From: Antoine Roux
To: Lottie Brooks
Subject: RE: RE: RE: RE: RE: RE: I love cheese

I have nine girlfriends at the present
moment of the clock.

PS The ostrich was sitting on me and peck
my eyeball. I suffocate nearly. I strongly tell
against to make a friendship with an ostrich.

Who has nine girlfriends and thinks that's normal?!?

What on earth am I meant to do now?!?!?!?!?

Thought about WhatsApping TQOEG to get their opinions but then I realized that if Amber found out she would tell EVERYONE, and I would look pretty stupid after all the Bugle boasting I'd been doing today. It was also pretty nice basking in the glory of having an HFB and TBH I'm not exactly keen to give that up . . . not just yet anyway.

There is a lesson here and it's **ALWAYS CHECK THE SMALL PRINT!**

NOTE TO SELF:
If there are any ostriches on the school trip, stay at least FIVE METRES away from them at ALL TIMES!

TUESDAY 20 SEPTEMBER

This morning Isha came running into registration excitedly. She clapped her hands together and announced, 'I've just spoken to Mr Lewis and it's definite. The school have agreed to have a girls' football team! Try-outs are next week!'

Jess and TSACG jumped up and joined in with the clapping.

'Are you going to try out, Jess?' Isha asked excitedly.

Jess grinned. 'Duh – of course!'

'How about you, Lottie?' she asked me.

'Nah, I'm terrible at sports,' I replied.

'I'm sure you're not, and they want to get people new to the sport involved too.' Isha opened her bag and pulled out an A4 poster that Mr Lewis must have made to recruit the new team. 'Look here – it says no experience necessary.'

I checked the poster; she was right. It did say no experience necessary. Plus, I started thinking about what Mum had said about trying to find some common ground with Isha, and what Jess had said about hanging out with her more.

'OK, sure – why not?' I said.

Isha smiled, and Jess gave me a little hug and said, 'Imagine if we all get in! It *would* be so much fun going to matches together!'

I smiled back. It *would* be fun to do something together like this and to get to know Isha better . . . but I'm just not quite sure I can imagine myself as a footballer?!

WEDNESDAY 21 SEPTEMBER

After mulling it over for a few days, I've decided that
I'm a bit cross with Antoine! His recent revelations have
definitely taken the shine off things a bit. I mean, I'm
still happy about the nice crisps he sent but I definitely
feel I've been a bit misled in the girlfriend-definition
area.

From: Lottie Brooks
To: Antoine Roux
Subject: NINE?!?!??!

Antoine,

I must admit that when I agreed to be your
girlfriend I had imagined that I would be the
only one. I'm not quite sure how I feel about
being one of nine, but it certainly doesn't
make me feel very special.

Who are they all and how do you even
remember their names?

Feeling a bit rejected,

Lottie (please note the lack of kisses)

PS I really enjoyed the bacon Bugles – they were very yummy. Monster Munch are still better though. FACT.

Let's see what he has to say to that!!

THURSDAY 22 SEPTEMBER

I have been thinking a lot about the girls' football team.
If I don't get in it, then there is a big risk that Jess and
Isha will become BFFs and Jess will forget ALL about me.

There is only one thing for it . . .

I **MUST** get into the team – **AT ALL COSTS!**

There is only one (quite big) problem with this: I know
nothing about football.

But it can't be that hard, can it?!

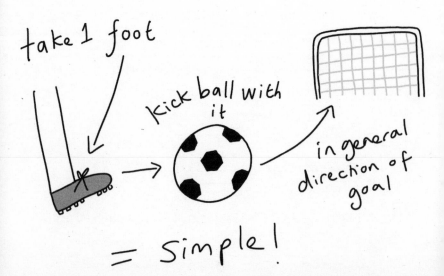

take 1 foot

Kick ball with
it

in general
direction of
goal

= simple!

I said to Toby at dinner, 'Why on earth all these Super League football players earn hundreds of thousands of pounds a week for doing something so easy, I don't know?!'

He said, 'The *what* league?'

'The Super League.'

'OMG, you are so DENSE – it's the Premier League. I bet you don't even know what the offside rule is either!'

I said, 'I do, actually.' Even though I didn't.

'What is it then?'

'It's where if you step over the white lines round the edge of the pitch, then you're out of the game.'

Dad and Toby both burst into fits of laughter.

'Lottie,' said Dad, 'it's not a game of musical chairs. It's a team game – you can't get told you're "out"!'

I said, 'I KNOW THAT! I'm just joking!' Even though I wasn't.

Anyway, who cares? Just because I'm not some sort of walking football rule book doesn't mean I'm not going to be a good player. I'll prove them wrong when I'm a Lioness playing for England and living in a multimillion-pound mansion with a swimming pool and a massive pond full of really expensive koi carp and a mega garage with twenty-four Ferraris in it and seventeen swimming pools and nine flamingos (zero ostriches though)! I'll be going on holidays to the Seychelles and the Maldives and they can carry on going to Soggy Beach in Wales – HA HA HA!

OOPS, I'm getting distracted. Let's get back to the task at hand . . .

Which was . . .

Ummmmmmmmmm . . .

Oh yes! Becoming a ~~Super~~ Premier League football player! So I've made a list of strategic strategies, which include:

(1.) Watch a football match on TV.

2. Watch 100 best all-time goals on YouTube.

3. Watch documentary on the Lionesses.

4. Read *Football for Idiots* book.

5. Meditate for an hour and visualize self as being REALLY EXCELLENT at kicking balls into nets.

Sounds simple enough, eh? I should be a football expert in no time!

NB When I say I must get into the team AT ALL COSTS, I didn't mean it literally . . . I'm not about to go out and commit a murder so that I can get into the team or anything. I just wanted to make that clear because if Mr Lewis or anyone trying out for the team dies in suspicious circumstances then I can say, hand on heart, that it definitely wasn't me.

I'm really not a violent person (unless it comes to Toby).

FRIDAY 23 SEPTEMBER

Tried Step One of my strategic strategy, which was watching a football match on the TV, but I had to turn it off after ten minutes because it was SO DULL!

I skipped to Step Six and ate a multipack of KitKat Chunkys while watching *Young Sheldon*, as I felt I deserved a reward anyway for putting myself through that mindless drivel.

Also read half a page of *Football for Idiots*, so I think that's enough footballing homework for one week.

Dad said that he thinks I should spend more of my time doing actual physical practice in the garden rather than just passive stuff that involves lying on the sofa, but what does he know? Yes, well, he may have been a football fan for forty-two years, played for Brighton's youth team and be an assistant coach on Toby's team, yada, yada, yada, but that doesn't mean he can go around bossing me about like he knows best!

Also, what he's failed to notice is that it's raining outside, and I don't like getting wet.

SATURDAY 24 SEPTEMBER

Now that I've completed ~~all most~~ some of my strategic
strategies (ahem) and am an expert on everything
football, it's time to get physical and put all that theory
into action!

The only problem was that the weather was still really
terrible, so I had to do more sitting on the sofa instead.

Dad came into the lounge and saw me and said, 'How on
earth do you expect to get a spot on the team if you've
never even played any football?!'

'It's still raining outside, Dad!'

'Football doesn't get cancelled because it's raining,
Lottie.'

'What if the players have just blow-dried their hair?!'

'Are you being serious?'

'I'm not sure – are *you* being serious?'

'Yes, if you want to get on the team, you need to learn how to kick a ball.'

'Can I take an umbrella?'

'NO!'

Wish me luck!

(12.15 p.m.)

While I was getting my trainers on, Dad said, 'Toby plays football. Why don't we ask him for some help too?'

Despite feeling like I'd rather die than ask my disgusting little brother for help, I had to admit it wasn't the worst idea Dad had ever had. The more people to practise with the better, I guess.

It turned out that Toby was keen to ~~show off~~ help but unfortunately the lesson didn't go very well. Kicking a ball is actually A LOT harder than it looks, and I discovered that my feet don't always seem to cooperate with what my brain tells them to do.

I don't know. Perhaps it was the pressure, but when I took a run-up to kick the ball I actually ended up kicking the grass/air more often than not. And then, even when I did manage to give the ball a decent kick, Dad and Toby were overly critical about which direction the ball went in. I didn't mean to destroy Mum's best hydrangea or smash Roger the creepy garden gnome, did I?!

Dad said, 'I bet even Bella is better at football than you, Lottie!'

I was like: 'LOL, yeh, right. Prove it!'

So, he did – and Bella actually nutmegged Toby. It was incredible . . .

Eventually everyone agreed that I had no natural skill whatsoever and decided to go back inside.

Toby said, 'I just don't think you are very sporty, Lottie. Perhaps it's best you go back to watching TikToks instead.'

How very rude!

PS I did go back to watching TikToks, but don't tell him that.

SUNDAY 25 SEPTEMBER

Oooh, got an email back from my supposed
'boyfriend' . . .

> Dearest Lottie,
>
> I feel horrified to the bone that I have led you
> into a confusing dark maze.
>
> I must hasty quick apologize. I thought
> you were aware of Antoine being VERY
> charming, funny and handsome, and
> therefore make an assume that I would have
> MANY love interests. It is now clear you are
> a total moron but worry not – you cannot help
> being born with only seven brain cells.
>
> You ask who my girlfriends are. They are
> Fleur, Noémie, Josephine, Veronique,
> Sophia, Lottie (that's you), one with blonde
> hair, one with strange-shaped head and one
> with an incredibly annoying laugh that sounds

like an old train (possibly called Julia). You
are correct. It is hard to remember – HA HA!

Please do not worry that you are not
special though – you are special to me,
just not THAT special.

Love of Antoine x

Feel VERY annoyed at him being so rude! Calling me a
moron and saying I only have seven brain cells – I must
have at least fifteen!!

MONDAY 26 SEPTEMBER

Football try-outs did not go to plan, which was absolutely, categorically NOT MY FAULT.

I mean, I scored the best goal of the entire match FGS (more on that later).

Let's start at the beginning. I was nervous all day long. I really wanted to do a good job as there was a lot riding on it – not only my friendship with Jess but my entire future career as a Lioness. And obviously, as you know, I'd done a huge amount of prep.

About thirty girls turned up to the try-outs and Mr Lewis said fifteen would make the squad. Then he split us into teams and asked us to decide between us which positions we would play. I knew there was a goalkeeper and ball kickers but apart from that I was pretty clueless, and I started to wonder if perhaps I should have read more than half a page of *Football for Idiots*. However, there was no time for regrets as we needed to get ready to play.

It quickly became clear that I was doing everything wrong – apparently I shouldn't scream when the ball comes near me; apparently I shouldn't squeal when I get mud flicked on me; apparently it's not OK to leave the pitch mid match to check your phone for messages; apparently it's not OK to eat a KitKat Chunky during the game (even if you are REALLY hungry).

It was SO strict and stressful!

When Mr Lewis blew the whistle, I was super relieved it was over. I never knew there was so much running involved! We all had a nice segment of orange for a refreshment and then Mr Lewis goes 'OK, second half!' and blew his whistle again.

I was like, WHAT?!

Turns out we had to do the whole thing again! WHY?!

I was quite dispirited at this point, but I figured that maybe it would probably go in my favour if I could show off some of my skills instead of mostly just squealing. I didn't have to wait too long before the ball came towards me.

Yes! I thought. *THIS IS MY MOMENT TO SHINE!*

I kicked the ball, and I couldn't believe it when it started
doing what I wanted it to do. I looked up and there
was nobody between me and the goal. I had a chance
to actually score! I started to run, and everyone else
was cheering. The opposition must have been so tired
because they couldn't keep up at all – in fact they were
mostly just standing still.

HA HA! I thought. *Obviously, everyone is shattered, and I
am the only one with any energy left!* *WATCH ME GO!* It
must have been that sneaky KitKat Chunky!

Me demonstrating my
<u>EXCELLENT</u>
footballing skills

Everyone else
shocked at my ability

Before I knew it, I was face to face with the goalkeeper. It was Isha. She looked really confused – was I the only one who had any idea how to play this game?! She sort of stood there not moving, so I slam-kicked that ball into the corner of the goal and then my hands went up into the air. Why was no one else cheering?! I had just scored the goal of my life!!! Well, technically the only goal of my life, but still.

Then Jess ran over and tapped me on the shoulder and said . . .

Oh, FGS!

Apparently we changed ends halfway through the game, but no one thought to tell me that! What I scored is actually called an 'own goal', so despite its sheer brilliance the point goes to the other team – how unfair is that?!

Basically no one gave me any credit **AT ALL** and, if anything, everyone seemed quite cross with me. I really hope this doesn't affect my chances of getting into the team.

TUESDAY 27 SEPTEMBER

Got home to another email from Antoine.

Chère Lottie,

Why are you no reply to Antoine? Are you still so sad to know that I have many romantic situations?

Please let me reassure you and feel some self-worth. Although I do indeed have many other girlfriends, listen to this fact: you are my number three favourite!

Congratulations!

Now for some advice – GET OVER IT!

Write back soon, my little dustbin,

Love of Antoine x

PS I am thinking of ending with Veronique as
she is as interesting as a spoon – so soon
there may only be eight of you x

First, I'm a moron, and now he is calling me HIS LITTLE
DUSTBIN?!?!

And then telling me I should just 'get over it'?! I mean,
where does this guy get off?!

On the flip side, I'm currently ranking 3/9 (or possibly 8).
I suppose that's sort of good news. I wonder where the
one with the strange-shaped head ranks?

(6.44 p.m.)

Decided to message my next-door neighbour Liv as she
always gives the best boy advice.

> **ME:** I have news. Antoine is now my
> HFB (Hot French Boyfriend).

> **LIV:** OOH LA LA!! Très Bon!

ME: Well, it would be Très Bon but there is a bit of a problem.

LIV: He's hot, he's French, he wants to be your boyfriend . . . What could possibly be the problem?

ME: Well . . . erm . . . it turns out I'm one of his 9 girlfriends. Is that too many do you think?

LIV: Erm, it's about 8 too many!

ME: ☹ What should I do?

LIV: Do you mind about him having so many girlfriends?

ME: Kinda.

LIV: Hmmm, well, my advice would be to dump him immediately because he is clearly not an HFB – he is in fact an HFLR.

ME: AN HFLR?!

LIV: A Hot French Love Rat!!

ME: Problem number 2 incoming . . .

LIV: OH GOD.

ME: I've already told everyone at school I have an HFB and if I dump him for being an HFLR and everyone finds out – they might think that HE dumped ME!

LIV: In that case I suggest going with Plan B. Ignore him for a bit and hope that he comes to his senses and dumps all the other ones.

ME: NICE! 🤞
Thanks, Liv x

LIV: Anytime, babes xx

WEDNESDAY 28 SEPTEMBER

SCHOOL TRIP NEWS!!

Today Mr Peters handed out forms about Camp Firefly.
We have to fill out our dietary preferences and also
which friends we would like to share a cabin with. You
can put down three people, but you're only guaranteed
to be with one of them.

The problem is who to put down. There are now five
of us in TQOEG, so that means each of us will have to
leave one person off the list and that's obviously going
to cause problems. Hmmm.

Mr Peters said we need to return our forms by the end
of next week, so we all have some thinking to do . . .

I am crossing all my fingers and toes that we all get
into a cabin together though, as that would be SO
MUCH FUN!

THURSDAY 29 SEPTEMBER

5.35 p.m.

Amber has been going ON and ON and ON about the friends lists.

I think it's better to keep your choices private, but Amber keeps asking what our choices are and then getting really angry when we don't tell her.

The thing is, I want to put Jess, Poppy and Molly on my list. I feel terrible leaving Amber off, but you can only put three people and basically the others are closer friends. Plus, they don't open their big mouths and blurt out private details about my love life when I have SPECIFICALLY told them not to.

Hopefully it won't matter anyway, because if we all put three members of TQOEG down each, then the easiest thing for the teachers to do would be to keep our group together.

But if Amber finds out that I left her off, I am DEAD MEAT.

TQOEG WhatsApp group:

AMBER: So I've been thinking about the friends lists for the cabins again and I reckon if everyone puts the same person down as their number-one choice, then we'd likely all get in a cabin together. So I'm happy to volunteer to be that person! Why don't you all put me down as your first choice?

POPPY: I don't think it works like that, Amber. The choices aren't in order of preference – you could get choice one or choice two or choice three.

AMBER: Well, maybe that's technically correct but I reckon teachers pay more attention to your first choice and surely everyone wants to be in a room with me right?

JESS: I think we should write down whoever we like, in whatever order we like, and then just cross our fingers that we all get in a cabin together!

MOLLY: Yeh, good idea, Jess. I won't take it personally if you guys don't put me. As Jess says: hopefully we will all be together anyway.

ME: Exactly. Let's not worry about who puts who. I'm pretty sure Mr Peters will make sure we are all together – he knows we are all BFFs.

AMBER: Well, I just think it doesn't hurt to have a strategy and I was trying to put myself forward, that's all. But it's a free world and if you don't want to put me on your list, then don't. You know me . . . I don't hold grudges . . . Just don't come crying to me when you get put in a cabin with Farty Freya or Sienna with the cheesy feet.

JESS: Thanks, Amber. Super sweet of you to be thinking of everyone else as normal.

AMBER: You're welcome

I mean, I think Jess was being sarcastic, but as usual it went right over Amber's head. I must admit I am very envious of her confidence.

8.27 p.m.

JESS: Ooh almost forgot to say – good luck for the football team announcement tomorrow. Apparently Mr Lewis is putting the list up on the gym noticeboard at 8.30 a.m.

ME: Eek, I'd almost forgotten. Do you seriously think I've got a chance?!

JESS: I really hope so. I mean, you did do some good kicking (even if it was in the wrong direction) 🤞 xx

FRIDAY 30 SEPTEMBER

I met up with Jess and Isha on the way to school and they talked excitedly about the team the whole way. They both said they were feeling nervous, but they didn't really seem it. I guess they knew that they had a great chance of getting in.

As we walked to the gym, we all wished each other luck, but I let them go in front of me to check the noticeboard first. They jumped up and down when they saw their names and then turned sadly to me when they saw that my name wasn't there.

'I'm really sorry, Lottie,' said Jess.

'Yeh, it sucks you didn't make the team too,' said Isha. 'It would have been a lot of fun.'

I sighed and tried to put on a brave face. My dream of being a Lioness for England was over before it properly began. ☹

It did not matter how brilliant my goal was (and it *was* brilliant); it seems that kicking the ball into the correct net was an essential part of the game. Personally I think, if that's a deal-breaker, they should put labels on the goalposts to make sure people don't get confused.

The worst thing about it is that my plan has totally backfired and now Jess and Isha will be spending EVEN MORE time together and getting closer and closer.

Suddenly, as if by magic, Angela the flying cabbage appeared and started flapping around by my ear . . .

'Shut up, Angela. You are not helping!' I said through gritted teeth.

'What's that, Lottie?' said Jess. 'Who's Angela?'

'Sorry, erm . . . just someone in my DT class.'

'I don't know anyone called Angela in –'

'Gotta dash or I'll be late for my lesson,' I shouted over my shoulder as I made a quick exit.

6.44 p.m.

> Poppy created group
> 'URGENT'

> Poppy added you

POPPY: Leah told Zariah that Millie told Beth that Sanjita told Chloe that TSACG are thinking of asking Isha to join their gang!

MOLLY: So?

POPPY: SO . . . have you not noticed that Isha and Jess are becoming good mates? If they get Isha, then maybe they'll try and steal Jess too? And then maybe Jess will put them all down on her friends list for Camp Firefly and our dreams of a TQOEG cabin will be OVER and EVERYTHING WILL BE RUINED.

MOLLY: Calm down, Poppy, you are being overdramatic.

ME: No, I think she's right. It's like Angela said – this is serious stuff!!!

MOLLY: Who's Angela?!

ME: Errr, she's a flying cabbage.

POPPY: No offence, Lottie, but we don't have time for your nonsense right now. We are too busy panicking.

ME: Fair point. So what shall we do first?

MOLLY: Scream. AHHHHHH!

AMBER: AHHHHHHHHHHHHHHHHHH!

ME: AHHHHHHHHHHHHH!

POPPY: Right, when everyone has finished screaming, we need to come up with a plan. Any ideas?

ME: Maybe we should invite Isha to join our WhatsApp group?

AMBER: WHOA! We can't just suddenly invite someone new into our WhatsApp group without careful consideration. It's a HUGE commitment. I mean, what if it doesn't work out? What if we aren't compatible?

POPPY: OK, OK, hmmm . . . Maybe we need to try and spend more time with her first – but that's difficult to do because it seems that TSACG have already got their claws into her.

MOLLY: There is another problem . . . Not sure if you knew this but TSACG have a USP.

ME: What is a USP?

MOLLY: A Unique Selling Point.

ME: SPEAK ENGLISH, MOLLY!

MOLLY: It means they have something unique about them that makes them stand out from their competitors, i.e. us.

POPPY: What do they have?!

MOLLY: Well, apart from obviously being sporty AND clever, they also have . . . branded T-shirts! I saw this picture on Lola's Instagram. She's the unofficial gang leader . . .

87 likes
BEST GANG EVER !!! ♥
TSACGTILLI DIE
Matchymatchy

AMBER: OMG I want one!

ME: What?! Why would you want a TSACG T-shirt when you are in TQOEG?!

AMBER: Errr . . . they look cool.

ME: ARGH this is a disaster – how are we going to compete with them when even our own gang members want a T-shirt?!

POPPY: Don't worry! We just need to figure out our USP . . . Any ideas?

No replies.

POPPY: OK, well, that's a great start. Maybe we should invite them both into town tomorrow? We could look at new clothes for the school trip and get a Frappuccino?

ME: Good call!

SATURDAY 1 OCTOBER

'This is even more urgent than we originally thought,' I said while we were standing in the queue at Starbucks.

'What? Why?' said Amber.

'Jess can't make it today . . . Any guesses why?'

'Ooh . . . I love games . . . My guess is that she is flying to Peru to take part in a table tennis tournament?' said Poppy.

'Maybe she's getting a new pet snake?' guessed Molly. 'Or maybe she's eaten a hundred doughnuts and can't get out of bed!'

'This isn't a game, guys,' I said. 'This is REAL LIFE! She can't make it because she and Isha are going over to Lola's for a sleepover!'

'Wow, those TSACG girls sure do move fast!' said Amber.

I nodded. 'Exactly, so we need a USP and we need it fast.'

When we had all collected our drinks, we headed over to a booth and I pulled out my notebook and pen. It was time for a brainstorm. This is what we came up with . . .

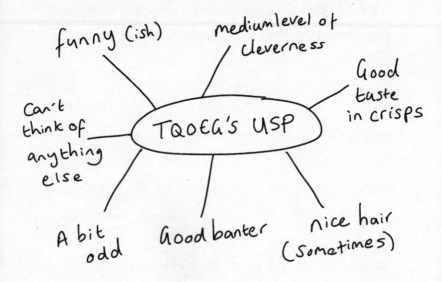

I personally thought our crisp game was our hottest USP, but I'll admit that it did sound pretty pathetic when you said it out loud. We all decided that there was nothing else for it – we needed MERCH too.

We discussed the pros and cons of water bottles, notebooks, pens, keyrings, magnets and hoodies – there are so many options out there. We pooled all our pocket money/spare change and the total budget came to £19.72.

Poppy decided to be our head of branding and went home to research options/costs. Apparently her uncle's friend runs a merchandising company, so they might be able to do us a deal – I'm looking forward to seeing what she comes back with.

MONDAY 3 OCTOBER

VERY BAD NEWS!

Next week we are having maths assessments. A test on Monday will be used to check that we are in the correct sets for our abilities. This is bad news for four reasons . . .

1. I HATE tests of ALL kinds but especially maths tests because you can't even try and blag them.

2. I suck at maths, like REALLY badly. It's my worst subject by far.

3. I'm worried I'll be moved down a set and then I won't be with Jess, and we already have hardly any classes together as it is.

4. I can't find my scientific calculator and Mum will go mad because that's the third one I've lost.

Mr Peters handed out some past test papers to look at – apparently we should know everything on them already but it's just to refresh our memories. I had a quick look at the questions, and I did not know anything already – in fact, I felt like I'd never seen any of this stuff before in my life. EEK.

When I got home, I told my parents I was stressing about the test and Dad suggested that maybe getting a maths tutor would help me if I was finding maths hard.

I said, 'WHOA there, big fella! Let's not get all hasty. I mean, yes, I'm a bit stressed, but I'm also a bit stressed about the fact that I think one of my ear lobes is a weird shape. It's all about context.'

TUESDAY 4 OCTOBER

And so it begins, my spiral into loneliness . . .

Jess and Isha had football training after school today,
Poppy and Molly had netball, and Amber had a date with
a boy called Zack from Eight Blue (if you count going to
the shop and buying chewing gum as a date).

Meanwhile, I have been ignoring Antoine for a full week
now and NOTHING! It's extra infuriating that I also
REALLY want to know if he has dumped Veronique yet . . .

I am tempted to email him to inform him that I'm
ignoring him (and ask him about Veronique), but I guess
that kind of defeats the point . . .

THOUGHT OF THE DAY:
Is it possible to ignore someone if
they are ignoring you back?

THURSDAY 6 OCTOBER

The Fun Police are going ON and ON about this stupid maths test like it's the most important thing in the universe. I mean, come on – there's more to life than quadratic equations. Like waffles with chocolate and squirty cream, for example . . . Mmmmmmm.

Unfortunately, they don't see it that way and they keep sending me to my room to revise. Mum has just come knocking on my bedroom door to ask how I'm getting on.

'Really great, actually,' I said. 'My brain feels like it's bursting with mathematical know-how.'

'I hope that's true, Lottie, because, although test scores aren't everything, it's important to work hard and try your best.'

'Take a chill pill, Mum! It's in the bag.'

'I beg your pardon?'

'Sorry . . . I mean, it's going great. I'm feeling much more confident about everything now!'

'Well, glad to hear it. I'll leave you to get on.'

'Oh, Mum, before you go – we don't have any waffles with chocolate and squirty cream, do we? This revising is hungry work and apparently waffles are good brain fuel.'

She laughed, even though I wasn't joking. But at least I'd got her off my back, which was good but also bad, because I've done absolutely nothing, and it is certainly NOT in the bag!

THOUGHT OF THE DAY:
It's not really my fault though . . . I mean, how can I be expected to revise when I'm so busy ignoring Antoine?!

FRIDAY 7 OCTOBER

We filled out our camp forms this morning and I didn't tell anyone my choices because I really don't want there to be any drama. Everyone was looking around the room nervously, trying to work out who'd put down who.

I also filled out my dietary requirements. Jess said that was just for people who have allergies or are vegan or whatever, but I thought it wouldn't hurt to put some ideas down (I do like to be helpful).

Camp Firefly

Name: Charlotte Rose Brooks
Friend choices: 1. Jess Williams
                2. Molly Lawrence
                3. Poppy Mills

Dietary requirements: No Veg
                      chicken nuggets
                      Don't like cottage pie
                      Daily bubble tea pls

Also, I think I might have an allergy to not having bubble tea, TBH. If I don't get one for a couple of weeks, my skin starts feeling a bit itchy and my right foot starts twitching.

I wonder if that's a legitimate medical condition. Maybe it's called lackofbubbleteaitus or something like that.

PS Still no reply from the HFLR.

PPS Still too busy ignoring him to revise.

PPPS My hair is greasy even though I washed it this morning – puberty is such a con!

SATURDAY 8 OCTOBER

URGH. Mum has printed out a bunch of maths worksheets for me to do.

I said, 'Mum, are you insane?! You can't expect me to do voluntary schoolwork at the weekend!'

'Well, it's not like you've got anything better to do, is it?'

'Untrue! I am planning on watching the entire season four of *Stranger Things* back to back.'

'You've already seen it twice!'

'But Jess has seen it three times and I need to get equal.'

She sighed. 'Look, Lottie – this is getting quite frustrating. You keep worrying that you aren't any good at maths, but you refuse to do anything about it!'

I said, 'Hmmm, yes. It's a bit like you worrying that you are getting super unfit and then making excuses as to why you can't go to the gym!'

She didn't have a comeback for that, so I will take that as a win!

7.06 p.m.

Much to my dismay, they are refusing to give up. At dinner Dad decided to start randomly calling out times tables. I must admit that I'm not the best at times tables – they make my brain start to plead with me.

When Dad asked, 'What is six times seven?' I swear I was just about to answer when the strangest thing happened . . .

A pretty weird way for Bella to say her first-ever words, if you ask me. We all ate dinner in silence after that, secretly worrying that Bella is some sort of freaky baby genius.

7.23 p.m.

Was making a Pot Noodle in the kitchen and Mum goes, 'What are you doing, Lottie? We've just had dinner!'

I said, 'It's not my fault – my brain told me to do it.'

She said, 'You are your brain, you doughnut!'

That only made me want a doughnut.

SUNDAY 9 OCTOBER

Tomorrow is D-Day. Or maybe we should say M-Day.

The dreaded maths test! **WA HA HAAAA!**

I think that if all subjects had parts in a film, then maths would play the big, bad, evil villain who you can't quite seem to kill.

A bit like this . . .

I looked through my bag and pulled out the crumpled test papers that Mr Peters gave us last week. I should have looked at them sooner, but I guess it's better late than never?

Or maybe it's not better, because I promise I did try. Unfortunately, the numbers started swimming around in front of my eyes and made my head hurt again, so I just snuggled up in bed with another Pot Noodle and watched some *Young Sheldon* to make myself feel better.

MONDAY 10 OCTOBER

7.45 a.m.

Over breakfast Mum said, 'Good luck today, Lottie. Why don't you take the test papers on your walk to school and you can double-check you're confident with everything on your way in?'

'Mum, I don't have time to look at it on the way to school. I'll be too busy talking to my friends.'

'OK, fine, but don't come crying to me when you can't answer any of the questions.'

Jeez, as if! Crying about a maths test would be mega pathetic.

4.04 p.m.

OK, so it turns out I am actually quite pathetic; I am crying over the maths test.

We got into class and each desk had a paper turned face down on it. Mr Peters told us there would be no talking and that we would have thirty minutes to complete the test. Then he looked at his watch and said, 'Starting now.'

I turned my paper over and as I looked at the questions I started to panic. I suddenly felt like I knew absolutely nothing. I looked around at everyone else and they were busy scribbling away – was I the only one who found maths hard?

I knew it was important to try though, so I took a few deep breaths and I tried to calm my nerves. I think I got some of the first questions right, but then they started getting more difficult and my brain wouldn't play ball. In fact, it felt like my brain was completely AWOL.

The time also went really quickly and when Mr Peters said, 'OK, you have five minutes left,' I still had over half the questions to do. Worse still, I could see that a few others had already finished – including Jess.

I rushed as fast as I could, but I just knew I had most of the answers wrong.

After Mr Peters had dismissed us, everyone started talking about how well they'd done, and I felt even worse. I didn't want anyone to know how hard I'd found it, so I just pretended it was OK – even to Jess . . .

When I got home, Mum asked me the same question and without really thinking I copied Jess's answer and said, 'Great – it was pretty easy as tests go.'

She gave me a squeeze and said, 'Excellent – well done, Lottie. I knew you'd smash it!'

I don't know why I lied. I guess I felt embarrassed to admit the truth – because I didn't 'smash it' as Mum had hoped. I barely even touched it. I barely gave it a light poke and then I ran away screaming.

Mr Peters said we'll get our marks back on Friday, so it won't be long until everyone finds out that I'm a stupid faker.

THOUGHT OF THE DAY:

I can't stop worrying about the test. I just know I did REALLY badly and now I'll get moved down a set and I won't be in a class with Jess. The worst thing is it's all my own fault. I should have listened to Mum and Dad and tried harder - they are going to be so cross with me when they find out!

WEDNESDAY 12 OCTOBER

OOH, positive news to report! Poppy just texted – the merch has arrived! She wouldn't tell us what she'd ordered because it's a surprise, but she's invited us over to her house tomorrow for the big reveal – exciting! I'm glad to have the distraction too because all I can think of is the impending doom of Friday. ☹

I wonder what she's got. I hope it's water bottles as I think they would be dead cool and everyone at school would be mega jealous.

THURSDAY 13 OCTOBER

We all gathered in Poppy's bedroom for the big reveal.
She was clearly super pumped to show us what she'd
ordered. She pulled out a big box and opened it slowly.
She took something out, then quickly turned round and
fiddled with her hair. Then she spun round.

We stared at her with open mouths.

Amber eventually broke the silence. 'What. Is. That?'

'It's a bopper headband!' said Poppy proudly.

We all looked at her blankly.

'You know . . . they wobble around when you move about . . .' said Poppy.

Molly shook her head in confusion. 'And how do you think that's going to help convince Isha to join our gang?'

Poppy sighed. 'They were in the sale, and it was the best I could do with a limited budget . . . Do you know how much water bottles cost?! Anyway, I think they're quite fun.'

'Yeh – if you're three years old!' said Amber.

Poppy sighed again. 'Anyway, that's not all –'

Oh, good! Here we go.

'If you spent £20, you also got ten free disposable ponchos.'

'So hang on,' said Molly. 'We're going to try and outdo TSACG – who've got their cleverness, their sportiness and their branded T-shirts – with . . . bopper headbands and a bunch of plastic ponchos?'

Poppy smiled. 'Yes! You are a hundred per cent correct – may the best gang win!'

God help us!

THOUGHT OF THE DAY:
Personally, I'd rather have a bopper headband than a boring old T-shirt, but I'll admit that I'm not the best person to consult on stuff like this.

FRIDAY 14 OCTOBER

Absolutely dreading today. I just HOPE, HOPE, HOPE my
mark is better than I expected. I would be super happy
with fifty per cent, but even that seems pretty unrealistic.
I'll update you later – please think lots of positive thoughts
for me!

Maths was the last lesson of the day, so I had all day to
worry about it, which was horrible. I could barely eat my
cheese panini at lunch I was so nervous.

But finally it was time for maths, so I walked in and slumped
down into my chair, trying to avoid Mr Peters's eyes.

'Right. Test results!' he said, clapping his hands together.
He picked up a stack of papers from his desk and started
slowly making his way round the classroom, handing
them out.

'Good work, Tia. Not bad, Ben. Nice improvement, Orla,' he muttered as he went. The mark was out of thirty and it was written in red biro at the top of the page, so it was difficult not to look at what other people got.

My heart was beating really quickly. *Please let me do OK, please!*

'Excellent, Jess . . . You too, Isha.'

I looked to my left and saw them grin at each other. I couldn't help myself glancing at their papers – they had identical scores of 25/30.

When Mr Peters got to my row, I crossed all my fingers underneath the desk. Soon he was standing in front of me – he found my paper and put it down on my desk.

'Lottie, some room for improvement here,' he said, raising an eyebrow.

I felt my cheeks flush as I saw the mark at the top . . .

I'd got 8/30! I was so embarrassed that I grabbed the paper and shoved it into my bag as quickly as I could – I really didn't want everyone to see it.

I spent the rest of the lesson trying to concentrate on not crying. Jess asked me a few times if I was OK and I just said, 'I'm fine.' When we were dismissed, I grabbed my bag and made sure I was the first out of the door. I knew everyone would be discussing their marks and that I probably had one of the lowest in the entire class.

Because it was the last lesson of the day, I ran home as fast as I could, so that I didn't have to face anyone. Luckily, my parents were distracted when I got in so I managed to swerve having to come clean to them – they are going to be so disappointed in me if they find out.

THOUGHT OF THE DAY:
Why does everyone else find maths so easy? Why do I find it so hard? I must be about as dense as a sea sponge. Oh God – I'm basically SpongeBob SquarePants!!

I may as well just give up school now and go and live in a pineapple under the sea and flip Krabby Patties for a living.

SATURDAY 15 OCTOBER

'Have you had your marks back for that maths test yet, Lottie?' Mum asked me while I was gloomily shovelling Shreddies into my mouth for breakfast. My heart immediately sank.

'Oooh, yes – how did you get on?' said Dad.

It may sound ridiculous, but I was really hoping they'd forgotten.

'I bet she's failed!' shouted Toby.

Bella blew a raspberry and bashed her teether on to her high-chair tray as if she was impatient to hear too.

I didn't want to let them down and I didn't want Toby to have the satisfaction of being right so before I knew what I was doing I'd said, 'I didn't fail. In fact, I got twenty-five out of thirty, which was one of the highest marks in the class.'

'Oh! My baby!' Mum cheered.

'We have a maths genius in the house!' said Dad.

'That's good, sis,' said Toby. 'I never knew you were clever.'

Bella let out an excited squeal and gave me a big gummy grin.

'Let's get a takeaway tonight to celebrate!' said Dad. 'Lottie can choose, and I won't even set a budget.'

Normally I would jump at the chance, but today I couldn't think of anything worse. I couldn't let him pay for a takeaway when I'd basically just stolen someone else's test score and pretended it was my own – could I?

So I said I wasn't feeling very well and then I spent the rest of the day in my room. I feel so ashamed of myself. I've lied to my whole family and if they knew the truth they'd be furious.

The worst thing is that I can't confide in anyone about

it because I don't want my friends to find out either. I can't speak to Antoine as I'm still ignoring him and he's obviously too busy with his other multiple girlfriends to care. And I can't speak to Daniel because he doesn't even want to know me any more. It all feels like such a mess.

SUNDAY 16 OCTOBER

6.23 a.m.

Feel like I barely slept last night. Every time I closed my eyes, I kept seeing Mum and Dad's happy faces and then I felt even worse. Angela was up to her old tricks too and buzzing around the room like a noisy mosquito!

Got a message from Jess:

> **JESS:** Hey, me and Isha have our first match at Nevill Rec today at 10. It's against Portslade Academy and they're meant to be really good. Fancy coming along to give us some moral support? XX

A good friend would go. A good friend wouldn't be jealous of her BFF for being sporty and clever and funny and kind and all the things I'm not. But I couldn't face it, not today.

I put my phone down – I'll reply later. I can't go on like this. I have to come clean. At the moment, the lie feels worse than the truth.

11.21 a.m.

Dad has taken Bella and Toby swimming, but I found Mum in the living room doing the hoovering.

I said, 'Mum, I've got something to tell you.'

'WHAT'S THAT, LOVE?' she said, shouting over the noise of the vacuum cleaner.

I took a deep breath. 'I'm not as clever as you all think.'

'SORRY? I CAN'T HEAR YOU!'

She switched the vacuum off, and I crumpled on to the sofa, crying.

'Mum, I have the IQ of a sea sponge.'

'What are you talking about, Lottie? Sea sponges don't have an IQ as they don't have brains.'

'EXACTLY!'

'You aren't making any sense, darling. What's wrong?'

'I didn't really get twenty-five,' I told her between sobs. 'I got eight. It was the lowest mark in the class, and I'll probably get moved down a set.'

'Oh, love.' Mum sat down next to me. 'Why did you lie?'

'Because I find maths really hard and I didn't want to admit it. I thought you'd think I was stupid and be disappointed in me.'

Mum hugged me. 'No! We'd never think that. Listen, I found maths difficult at school too, so you're certainly not alone, you are certainly not stupid, and you are certainly not SpongeBob SquarePants. OK?'

I breathed a sigh of relief. 'So, you're not angry?'

She raised her eyebrows and gave me a serious look. 'Well, I can't say I'm not frustrated that you didn't put more effort into revising, Lottie. You kept reassuring me you knew it and you had it covered.'

'I know . . .'

'We can't all be good at everything, but it's still important to ask for help if you need it. Burying your head in the sand is not the answer.'

I felt tears stinging my eyes – she was being so nice to me, even though I probably didn't deserve it.

'Thanks, Mum.'

She gave me another hug. 'That's all right, but no more lying, OK? We love you just the way you are – remember that.'

'I promise.'

Then, even though she was mid hoover, we snuggled

up together under a blanket and watched some of
Sunday Brunch. That's a big thing for Mum – she does
love to hoover!

(**8.22 p.m.**)

Later on, when Dad, Toby and Bella got back, Mum must
have taken them to one side and told them about it
because no one mentioned it at all. I was really relieved as
I was dreading Toby making fun of me, but he didn't.

When I said goodnight before I went up to bed, Dad gave
me an extra-long cuddle. 'Listen, love, me and your mum
were thinking – maybe it might be a good idea to get a maths
tutor. Some one-on-one time to help you get up to speed?'

As much as dedicating any more spare time to maths
seemed like a crazy idea, I had to admit he was probably
right.

'OK, Dad,'

'Great,' he said excitedly. 'Did you know that Jean your
babysitter used to be a maths tutor? Maybe me and your

mum could go on a few more date nights and she could tutor you while we are out? That way everyone's a winner.'

Inside, I felt absolutely horrified at the prospect, but I didn't have a leg to stand on, did I?! So I nodded and did my best fake grin.

'Brilliant. That's settled then!' he said.

'Night, Dad.'

'Night, Lotts.'

Just as I was about to leave, he pulled me in for another squeeze . . .

MONDAY 17 OCTOBER

Mr Peters asked me to stay behind after registration this morning. He asked if I'd been struggling to keep up with the work in maths and I admitted I had. He asked if I thought that maybe moving sets could be wise, so that I'd feel more confident in class and be doing work that's at the right level for me. I had never thought about it that way, but maybe he's right, so I said I thought that sounded like a good plan.

I also came clean to the girls about my real test scores and they were all really kind and supportive. The good news is that I'll be moving into Poppy's class, so it's not like I'll be alone. Apparently the teacher is super nice and explains things really well. Poppy said she isn't the best at maths either, but she doesn't seem bothered about it.

THOUGHT OF THE DAY:

I feel so much better about everything today. All the pressure I was putting on myself wasn't worth it. The only real downside now (apart from Jean the Mean Machine tutoring me – although I hope Dad may forget about that!) is that I won't be with Jess any more, and I already feel like I hardly get to hang out with her as it is. Basically I miss her.

TUESDAY 18 OCTOBER

Today was the day we decided that we would officially ask Isha to join TQOEG. We were all excited (and a bit nervous) about presenting her with our slightly bonkers merch, but it was all over before it had even begun – because when we walked into registration this is what we saw . . .

We were literally seconds too late – gutted. Poppy quickly shoved the box of merch under the desk before anyone saw. I mean, maybe it was for the best? We'd have probably made total fools out of ourselves – to the average person, the bopper headbands were pretty cringe. I couldn't help but worry that, with Isha joining TSACG, maybe it wouldn't be long before they lured Jess away too.

We must have all looked a bit down after school because when we saw Jess she came running over and said, 'Hey, guys, what's up? You look kind of sad.'

'Nothing,' I said quickly. 'Where's Isha?'

'Isha? Oh, I guess she's with her new gang. Did you hear? She joined TSACG. What's in the box?'

'Um . . . it's just an erm . . . science project?' said Poppy.

Unfortunately, one of the stars had escaped through the top of the box so Jess started to pull it out. 'OMG!! Bopper headbands! These are so cool!!'

'Are they?!' said Molly.

'Yes!' said Jess. 'They're adorable! Where did you get them?'

'I ordered them,' said Poppy proudly.

'We thought they were a bit lame . . .' said Molly.

Jess put the headband on. 'Nah, I love them. Did you know that TSACG have T-shirts? Pretty boring, if you ask me.'

I laughed. She was SO right. Why had I ever doubted it?

We all put the headbands on and started to walk home, arm in arm, and it felt so good. Halfway back it started to rain.

'Urgh, shall we hide in Saino's until it stops?' said Jess.

'No need,' said Poppy. 'I also have these!'

Then she pulled out the disposable ponchos and we carried on walking home, probably looking like total weirdos – but who cares?!

Later on, while I was in my room doing my maths homework (I know, I know, I'm a changed lady!) my phone started ringing. Jess was FaceTiming me, so I pressed 'accept'.

'Erm . . . so what's the goss?' I said.

Jess laughed. 'What, since I last saw you about forty-five minutes ago?

'Yep!'

'Not much,' I said. 'Just doing my homework.'

'Are you feeling OK, Lottie?!'

That made me laugh. 'I'm glad you liked the bopper headbands, Jess. I was a bit worried you'd think they were silly.'

'Like them? I **LOVE** them! I'm still wearing mine.'

She brought the top of her head into view and started jiggling around, making the stars dance.

I smiled. I wasn't going to mention anything about the real reason why we got them, but it just felt right. 'We were a bit worried you might join the other gang with Isha . . .' I said slowly.

'Who?! TSACG?! Are you insane?'

'I think I am . . . a bit.'

'Well, all the best people are,' said Jess. 'But I know one thing for sure . . . I'm TQOEG till I die!'

I don't think I'd ever felt so relieved.

'Anyway, let's get down to business and the real reason I called,' she said.

'Oh, yeh. What's that?'

She balanced her phone on her desk and put a packet of digestives in front of her. 'Biscuit Face Challenge, of course. Proceed directly to the kitchen and select the weapon of your choice.'

She didn't have to ask twice! I leapt down the stairs two at a time and grabbed a packet of Jammie Dodgers.

FRIDAY 21 OCTOBER

No one could concentrate in lessons today as all people could talk about was the trip. What clothes to bring, what snacks, how much spending money, and of course the all-important question: who would be in your cabin?

Mr Peters said that he wouldn't be revealing the cabin allocations until we arrived at Camp Firefly, but that didn't stop me and the girls asking him a couple of times (very subtly, of course).

SATURDAY 22 OCTOBER

Dad looked after Toby and Bella so that me and Mum could go into town and do some shopping for the trip. I got a pair of new jeans, a waterproof jacket and a lovely soft hoodie (for ages fourteen to fifteen because I like them big and snuggly).

Then we went to Boots to get toiletries. Mum suggested getting dry shampoo in case I don't get time to wash my hair, and I also got two cans of deodorant because we'll be doing lots of physical stuff and I might get extra sweaty. We also bought a box of tampons and a pack of sanitary towels – my periods seem to be kind of regular now so I don't think I'll get one at camp, but I also don't want to get caught short, as Mum would say. Plus, you never know – some of the girls in my cabin could forget to bring them; Jess hasn't even had her period yet! She doesn't seem to care though.

After we'd finished shopping, Mum suggested going to a cafe to warm up as it's been getting colder lately. We went to Starbucks, and I got a large hot chocolate (with

cream and marshmallows, natch) and Mum got a latte.
I told her I'm never going to drink coffee, even when I'm
an adult, and she laughed.

Now, I'm back home lying on my bed writing this and
I'm feeling a little sad. I had such a lovely day spending
time with Mum that I'm feeling a bit wobbly again about
going away. Four nights away does feel like a REALLY
long time.

THOUGHT OF THE DAY:
Oh gosh, PLEASE, PLEASE, PLEASE let
me and Jess be cabin mates! I've missed
her so much and it will be the perfect
opportunity to get our friendship
properly back on track.

SUNDAY 23 OCTOBER

Spent the morning packing. Mum made me stick name labels on every item of clothing I was taking – even my underwear!

I said, 'Mum, why would anyone try and steal my pants?!'

And she said, 'You'd be surprised, Lottie!'

Like what does that even mean?!

The worst part of all is that she had the name labels made when I was in Year Three, so not only do they say my full name on them but they also have a picture of a unicorn next to it. **MEGA CRINGE**.

I told her that Year Eights are not into having unicorns on their knickers, but she said it was wasteful to throw them away and I'd have to wait until they'd run out before I could choose a more age-appropriate favourite animal!

I tried to explain that soon-to-be teenagers don't really like animal stickers in their pants AT ALL and she just laughed. Hmph.

I bet she'll still be nagging me to label my underwear when I'm twenty-five.

12.45 p.m.

Oh, great. Bella has come to help me pack and when I say 'help', I mean 'be REALLY annoying'.

I suppose I should be glad she's not trying to terrorize the hamsters again.

1.13 p.m.

Oh, wait. I spoke too soon!

7.23 p.m.

Right – I'm all packed and ready to go! I hope that I haven't forgotten anything. I made a list to make double sure and I've taken . . .

* Jeans

* Denim shorts

* Hoodies (2)

* Trackie Bs

* T-shirts (4)

* Pyjamas

* Socks (4 pairs)

* Knickers (6 pairs – inc. 2 for emergencies!)

* Bras (2)

* Waterproof coat

* Trainers (1 old pair and 1 new pair)

* Towel

* Toiletries

* Hairbrush

* Hairbands

* Make-up (mascara, concealer, lip gloss, blusher)

* My favourite fleecy blanket

* Teddy One-Eye (Yes. I know I'm twelve years old but I might miss him! I've stuffed him right at the bottom of my suitcase, just in case I need a little cuddle.)

And now the most important part . . . SNACKS! I have:

* KitKat Chunky multipack (4 bars)

* Pickled-onion Monster Munch multipack (6 bags)

* Sugar-free chewing gum (1 tub, strawberry flavour)

* Sour belts (3 packs, watermelon flavour)

* Wotsits Giants (1 packet)

* Apples (3)

(I didn't want the apples, but Mum made me put some fruit in. I will put them in the bin as soon as we arrive.)

Right, I'd better go and do my final checks, but don't worry – I'm packing my diary too so I can keep you updated along the way. This is my first proper trip away from home and I don't want to forget a single thing!

(8.04 p.m.)

I just checked my email because I won't get a chance to do it for the next week. I guess I must have been hoping to have received something from Antoine because I couldn't help feeling disappointed that all I had was an email from my 'Great-Uncle Bartholomew' informing me that I was the sole heir to a £3.5 billion fortune. I got excited when I first read it, but then I remembered Mum telling me that those messages are always a scam (which is a shame as I could have used £3.5 billion – think of all the bubble tea it could buy!).

I'm not even sure why I'm disappointed not to have heard from the HFLR . . . I know I could do SO much better, but I just thought that he'd care enough to wish me a good trip. Oh well, his loss – au revoir, Antoine! I hope you have a ~~terrible~~* mediocre life.

*I crossed out the 'terrible' because that felt a bit harsh. I mean, maybe 'mediocre' does too, but you can't seriously expect me to want him to become an Oscar-winning actor or an F1 racing-car driver, can you?!

9.25 p.m.

Mum came in to tell me to turn my light off and go to sleep and I burst into tears. I don't even know where it came from. I was snuggled in my bed and suddenly realized that for the next few days I had no idea what kind of bed I would be sleeping in and there would be no one to come and tuck me in.

'Oh, love, what's wrong?' asked Mum.

'I just . . . I just . . . I don't know if I want to go. I know this sounds so silly because I'm at high school now, but I'm really going to miss you.'

She gave me a big hug and started stroking my hair. 'It doesn't sound silly at all. You've never been away from home before and we're all going to miss you too, but you're going to have so much fun.'

'But what if I get really homesick?' I said.

'Do you remember what we used to do when you were little and you got nervous before school or nursery?'

I wiped my eyes with my pyjama sleeve and shook my head.

Mum stood up and went over to my desk and picked up a pen, then she sat back down on my bed and drew a little heart on the inside of her wrist.

I smiled as the memory came flooding back. I gave her

my arm and she drew an identical heart on my wrist.

'What does this mean?' she asked, tapping the hearts.

'It means, whenever I miss you, I just need to look at the heart and know you're right there with me, loving me as always.'

'Exactly! You can do this, Lottie Brooks. I know you can!'

'Thanks, Mum.'

OK, I'm switching my lights off now. I need to get some sleep as I have a big day tomorrow! Byeeeeee x

MONDAY 24 OCTOBER

6.57 a.m.

I'm up really early because we need to be at school
for 8.30 a.m. Check me out – I look like a total profesh
outdoorsy person, don't I . . . ?

Bear Grylls,
eat your
heart out!

It's about a three-hour drive to Camp Firefly so we also
have to bring a packed lunch to eat on the journey.
I really hope that I get to sit next to Jess or Poppy or
basically anyone who isn't likely to vomit all over me.

9.04 a.m.

We're on the coach.

I had an emotional goodbye with the fam. I even hugged Toby, which was kind of weird/gross.

I'm writing this very quickly as I don't want anyone to see, but I just had to let you know that Amber arrived late and she had to sit next to Burger Tom in our coach, who is already sitting on a seat covered with an M&S carrier bag. HAAAAAA!

He also has a stack of brown-paper sick bags on his lap, and we're all taking bets on how many he will use.

Jess votes two; Poppy votes three; Molly votes five. I'm going with a wildcard guess of seven!

9.10 a.m.

All the teachers are wearing normal-people clothes like jeans and sweatshirts. They almost look like actual human beings – it's SOOOOOO strange!!

Tom is already looking a bit green, TBH. Now I'm wondering if seven voms may have been a bit conservative!

Oops, there we go. The driver took a roundabout a bit too quickly and Number One is in the bag!

Number Two has landed, closely followed by Number Three. Amber is absolutely screeching at Mr Peters to be moved, but unfortunately the coach is full.

Voms Four and Five have occurred – some came out of his nostrils. The coach absolutely stinks!

Mr Peters has reluctantly switched seats with Amber
after she pretended to faint. Got to hand it to her – it was
a nice tactic.

Oops, there goes Vom Number Six – it was a forceful one
and a little bit splashed out of the bag and hit Mr Peters
on the arm. He looks as if he is trying REALLY hard to be
sympathetic but not quite managing it.

11.55 a.m.

All that puking must have tired Burger Tom out because he's now asleep. I am half relieved because the air in the coach was starting to turn toxic, but also half annoyed that I only needed one more chunder to win.

12.02 p.m.

Attempted to eat my packed lunch, but Mum had made me a tuna sandwich and the smell of it made me want to heave. Apparently we are nearly there, which is good, as we all desperately need some fresh air.

3.35 p.m.

We have arrived! Well, we arrived ages ago, but I'm just getting the chance to fill you in now because it's been really busy.

SO . . .

We had **SEVEN VOMS!!!!!!!!!**

We pulled up in the car park and Burger Tom was sick all over the steps when he was getting off the coach, so I win – hurrah!

The downside of this was that everyone had to step over it as they tried to get off. Mostly people managed OK, except for Amber, who skidded in it and got it on her fave Air Force 1s. She was not happy.

Then, as the drivers were unloading our bags, we saw another coach arrive.

'Who are they?' I asked Jess.

'No idea . . . Maybe it's another school . . .' she replied.

For some reason, I'd assumed that our school would be the only one here. We must have all been looking a bit confused because Mr Peters said, 'Ahhh, that will be the Willow Park College girls.'

'The Willow Park College girls? I don't like the sound of them,' said Amber a bit too loudly.

Mr Peters got all stern at her. 'Excuse me, Miss Stevens. I don't want to hear you talking like that. Kingswood High does not own this camp. We are lucky to have such a wonderful school joining us for the week. In fact, I may go and speak to their teachers and see if they would be interested in doing some activities together – I think it would be great for us all to join forces!'

After he'd walked off to chat to the teacher in charge, Poppy said, 'What I want to know is where are the Willow Park College boys?'

'DUH, it's obvs an all-girls school,' replied Molly.

We watched as the girls filed off the coaches. They were all dressed in school gold-and-navy PE kits – unlucky!

'Well . . . I don't care what Mr Peters says. I don't like the look of them – they have a bad vibe,' said Amber.

'You can't say that based on what they look like,' said Jess. 'They could be really nice.' She took a couple of steps towards their coaches and gave a big wave.

The girls stared right at us with stony faces. The tallest one, who had long blonde hair in a plait and a small, pointy nose, whispered something to the group standing with her. Then they all started laughing before turning their backs on us.

Poor Jess looked utterly dejected. Got to love her for trying though.

'What did I tell you?!' said Amber triumphantly. 'They have **BAD VIBES** written all over them.'

For once, I had to agree with her.

'Right,' said Mr Peters. 'Let's get moving, shall we?'

He led us out of the car park to
a picnic area. Beside the picnic
area was a basketball court, and
that was surrounded by rows
of wood cabins. They looked
kind of cosy and cute so I smiled to myself, thinking how
much fun it would be living in them for the next few
days.

'OK, sit down at the picnic tables, everybody. I have a few
housekeeping announcements to make while you finish
your packed lunches,' said Mr Peters. 'Firstly, some good
news – I've spoken to Miss Moulson, the head of Year
Eight at Willow Park College, and she would love to mix
our groups up a bit this week.'

I think he must have heard a collective sigh from TQOEG
because he gave us a warning look and said, 'And I know
you will be VERY friendly and helpful towards them.
Remember that your behaviour is a direct reflection on
Kingswood High and I hope you will do the school proud.
Anyway, down to the important business – cabins! I
know you are all desperate to find out who you are
sharing with, so I'll put you out of your misery . . .'

OMG! HERE COMES THE DRAMA LLAMA!!!!

Contrary to popular belief I'm actually pretty chill.

Everyone started getting dead nervous and I crossed both sets of fingers behind my back and prayed that TQOEG would all be together. The cabins each slept five or six people so I was really hoping it would work out perfectly . . .

Mr Peters started calling out our cabins, one by one. They're all named after wild animals and outdoorsy stuff like Lazy Bear, Mountain Top, Flying Eagle and Wander Inn – cool, huh?

'In Whistling Woods will be Poppy, Jess, Isha –'

AND ME, AND ME!! I hoped.

'Chloe and Kylie.'

NOOOOOOO!

My heart absolutely sank.

'In Shooting Stars, we have Amber, Molly, Lottie, Ella and Mia.'

Everyone around me was jumping up and hugging their cabin mates and I tried not to look disappointed. I didn't want Molly and Amber or any of the other girls to think I didn't want to be with them; it's just that obviously I was really hoping to be with ALL my friends.

I smiled as best as I could and picked up my bags. Out of the corner of my eye, I could see Jess, Poppy and Isha squealing and hugging. What hurt the most was the realization that Jess probably put Isha on her friendship list instead of one of TQOEG. This trip was supposed to be about me and her spending some quality time together.

BZZZZZZZZZZZZ. BZZZZ. BZZZZZZZZZZZZZZZZZZ.

Oh, for goodness' sake. Why won't Angela leave me alone?!

Jess, Poppy and Isha must have seen me looking sad as they all came running over.

'It's a shame we aren't in the same cabin, Lottie,' said Poppy.

'Yeh, I was really hoping that Mr Peters would keep us all together,' agreed Jess.

'Me too,' I said sadly.

'Don't worry, Lottie. I'm sure there'll be plenty of spare time for us all to hang out,' said Isha.

They were being kind and trying to cheer me up – only it wasn't working. It could have been perfect; it *should* have been perfect. Except, as is often the case with my life, **it wasn't**.

As everyone started gathering their bags and suitcases, I hung back to speak to Mr Peters. In my heart I knew that it probably wouldn't help, but I just HAD to give it a shot.

He saw me standing next to him. 'Everything OK, Lottie? You know which cabin you're in, right?'

'Yes, sir. It's just . . . I . . . I really wanted to be with Jess and Poppy. Is there any chance I could switch cabins?'

'I'm afraid not, Lottie. If I let you switch cabins, it wouldn't be fair because everyone else would start asking to switch too. I did say that it wasn't guaranteed that you'd get everyone on your friendship list.'

'I know, sir. I just was really hoping we'd be together . . . They're my best friends, you see.'

'Look, Lottie, part of this trip is about trying new activities and making new friends. If we put you in cabins with *all* your closest friends, then it wouldn't really be the same experience, would it?'

'I guess not, sir,' I said reluctantly.

'I understand you're disappointed, but don't let it put a dampener on things. We're going to have a great time and there will be plenty of time to see Jess and Poppy in between activities and in social time. OK?'

'OK, sir.'

'Good, now grab your bag and get going. If you don't catch up with them, you'll end up with the worst bunk,' he said, winking at me.

OH GOD. I hadn't thought of that!

I grabbed my case and started to run, but they were

already pretty far ahead and by the time I caught up
with them, puffing and panting, they'd already flung
their things on to their chosen beds, leaving me with
the least favourite option . . . Yep, you guessed it: bottom
bunk nearest the loo.

Ella and Mia were sharing the other
bunk and Amber had nabbed the
prize spot of a single bed opposite
the bathroom. I obviously looked

disappointed as she said, 'Sorry, Lottie, but you snooze,
you lose!' Then she jumped off her bed and started
unpacking her case, hanging up the huge amounts of
clothing she had brought with her.

I flung my case under my bunk and sat down on my
mattress. There didn't seem much point unpacking, TBH.
Molly hung her head down over the top.

'At least you get me as a bunk-bed mate!' she said,
smiling. 'That means we get to share a wardrobe too – or
snack cupboard, as I like to call it.'

She jumped off the bunk, checked the others were

busy unpacking and then put her fingers to her lips . . .
'Shhhhhh,' she said, opening our wardrobe door.

I could not believe it. She'd brought even more
contraband sweets and chocolate than me!

'How on earth did you manage to smuggle in all this
stuff?' I asked.

'Easy – I just prioritized snacks over clothes,' she said.

'Same,' I replied, laughing. 'I knew there was a reason we
were BFFs.'

She put her arm round me. 'I'm gutted we're not all in
the same cabin too, but we're going to have the best
time, I promise.'

We shared a pack of strawberry laces and had a Mars Bar
each, and now I'm lying on my bed writing this while we
have a bit of chill-out time before dinner.

My bunk will be OK, I think. I mean, I may be nearest the
toilet, but at least I'm with girls. It'll be a lot better than

using the bathroom after Toby anyway . . . So little of his wee seems to end up in the toilet that sometimes I think he just flings the door open and wees from the doorway!

My bed also seems pretty comfy as beds go. Everyone has a white duvet and a white pillow, and each pair of bunk beds has a wardrobe next to it to share. It might be all right living in Shooting Stars cabin for the next few days.

OOH, hang on – Mr Peters just knocked and it's time to gather on the basketball court because we're going to have a tour of the camp before going to the canteen for dinner.

BRB x

So – camp is REALLY cool!

From the cabins it's about a ten-minute walk away to the sports hall, where we will do all our indoor activities. Next door to that is a shop where we can buy sweets and souvenirs, and the canteen where we have all our meals. Then there is a big lake for the water-based stuff, woods to explore, a playing field and a campfire area. The other outdoor activities are spread around the grounds, which are HUGE.

I've drawn a little map for you so you can get your bearings . . .

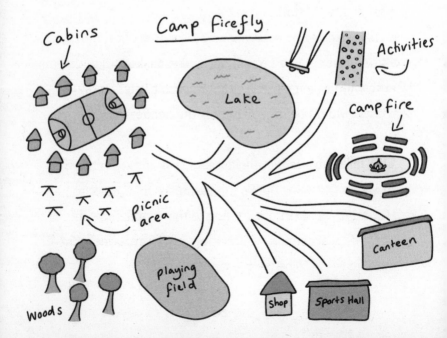

After the tour, it was time for dinner. I was really hoping it would be something I liked, as I'd only had two Mars Bars, a KitKat Chunky and three bags of Monster Munch since I'd arrived and I was starving.

It ended up being great because the canteen was a bit like school, where you get a tray and wait in line to ask for what you'd like from the dinner ladies. Luckily, there were a few options, and I went for fish and chips, and then apple crumble and custard for pudding. YUM. It was much better than being at home because we never get proper puddings like that, except sometimes on a Sunday.

Now to the most important part . . .

After dinner, we had to gather on the basketball court and stand in our cabin groups. Then Mr Peters told us that we would be meeting our group leaders.

OMG!!!!!!! Ours is just the cutest!

He came over to introduce himself and said in a cute Australian accent, 'Hey, Shooting Stars, my name's Kai and I'm going to be your leader this week.'

'Hiiiiii, Kaiiiiii,' we all said in unison. Then we all stared at him open-mouthed because he was SO GORGEOUS!

Even Amber was totally lost for words, and I've NEVER seen that happen before.

After about five seconds, he laughed and said, 'Well, it's great to meet you, guys. I'll be taking you round the activities and making sure you get there on time and do everything safely. So do any of you have names?'

Then Amber goes: 'I do. I have a name.'

And we all absolutely cracked up and she went bright red. I was absolutely loving it because, as we all know, that's usually the type of thing that happens to me.

Kai smiled a gorgeous smile. 'Okaaaaay . . . that's great to hear you have a name. Any idea what it might be?'

Luckily, Molly bailed her out.

'She means her name is Amber. And I'm Molly – you're Australian, right?'

'Yup! Sydney born and bred!'

'Cool. I lived in Sydney for a while – it was very hot!'

Kai laughed. 'Yeh, we do get *slightly* better weather over there. I'm still trying to get used to it here, which is why I normally wear two jumpers!'

After we'd all introduced ourselves, Kai told us a bit more about himself. Here is a picture of him and some fun facts . . .

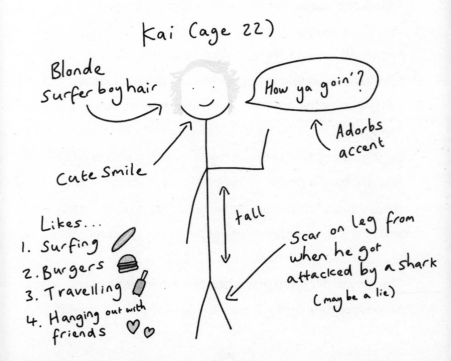

Next, it was time for our evening activity, which was a campfire.

We walked past the lake to a big circle surrounded by benches. As we all sat down, the leaders handed out mugs and then the dinner ladies came round with huge flasks of the most delicious hot chocolate I have ever tasted. Or maybe it tasted so delicious because it was getting late and cold, and it was so much fun sitting outside in the dark with my friends. Whatever. We were also given two giant marshmallows each (one pink, one white), and because the chocolate was steaming hot, they all melted on top of it – SO GOOD!

I really enjoyed the campfire. We sang loads of funny songs – some I knew and others I had to learn the words for: 'Alice the Camel', 'Boom Chicka Boom', 'Ten Green Bottles', 'Gin Gan Gooli' and my favourite, which was 'If You're Happy, and You Know It'. That one was so super cheesy and a bit babyish, but we shouted it so loud and did all the actions that it was actually pretty funny.

The only bad bit was that when the songs finished and we were getting up to go back to our cabins Molly goes,

'Ewww, Lottie, what is that stuck in your hair?'

I put my hand to the end of my ponytail, and I felt a
sticky lump of marshmallow in it.

'What?! How did that get there?'

Then I heard some giggling from the benches behind us. I
spun round and came face to face with a group of Willow
Park College girls, including Pointy Nose.

Without waiting for an answer, she smirked and walked off.

'What a cow!' said Amber.

'Do you think they did that on purpose?' asked Jess, looking shocked.

'Jess, you are so naive – they one hundred per cent did that on purpose,' said Amber, putting her hands on her hips. 'But I don't think they understand who they're messing with!'

I sighed. Like Jess, I wanted to believe it was an accident but, from the way they'd acted so far, it didn't seem very likely.

When we got back to the cabin, Molly helped me get as much of the marshmallow out of my ponytail as possible, but it was really difficult so we had to snip some of the strands off. I don't think you can notice it too much, but that's not really the point.

I just really, REALLY hope we don't have to do any activities with Pointy Nose and her crew tomorrow.

Just got a message from Mum . . .

> **MUM:** Hey you, how's it going? I hope you've settled in and had a nice day? Love you, Mum xx

> **ME:** Hey, Mum! It's nice here. I'm a bit sad because I didn't get into a cabin with Jess and Poppy but I'm with Molly and Amber so it's OK. There is another school here called Willow Park College and we are going to be doing activities with them tomorrow.

> **MUM:** Glad to hear that, love. Don't worry about the cabins. I'm sure you'll get lots of time to hang out together and you might make lots of new friends with the other school too. What did you have for tea?

ME: Fish and chips. It was good but not as good as yours! We have room inspection in 15 minutes, so I've got to tidy up now! Love you, nunnite Xx

MUM: OK, love. Have the best time tomorrow! Love you, nunnite Xx

I thought about telling her about the marshmallow incident, but then I thought maybe it would just make her worry and hopefully I can stay out of Pointy Nose's way for the rest of the trip anyway.

I switched my phone off and felt a little down. I rubbed the heart on my wrist and felt a tear prick in my eye. It was nice hearing from Mum, but suddenly she felt very far away, and I miss her. Everything here feels and smells different to my house. I kind of wish I had my own pillow and duvet to snuggle up in. At least I have my fleecy blanket and Teddy One-Eye.

'Lottie! What are you doing just lying there?! We have room inspection in a few minutes – you've got to help tidy up!' shouted Molly, interrupting my thoughts.

She's right. Our cabin is a state – if Mr Peters sees this we're toast!

10.15 p.m.

EEEK! We scored 5/10 on the room inspection. Me and Molly got into trouble for not unpacking and the worst part was that, after he'd told us off for our mess, he wrote the score on a board outside our cabin, so now everyone else can see how badly we did too.

Then he came round with a box and got us to put our phones in it because they don't trust us not to stay up with them all night. So annoying.

Molly asked, 'What if one of us has a medical emergency and we need to call an ambulance?'

Mr Peters sighed and said, 'Well, what sort of medical emergency are you planning on having, Molly?'

'I could be climbing up to my bunk and then accidentally slip and decapitate myself on one of the rungs of the ladder?'

'Well, I'm sorry to break it to you, Molly, but I don't think even the best doctor in the world would be able to sew your head back on. Plus, I think slipping on a ladder is much more likely to result in a splinter and I don't think anyone would take too kindly to you dialling 999 for that. Instead, I'd suggest knocking on my cabin door, which is four doors down on the right. OK?'

'OKKKKKKAAAAAY, sir,' we said, reluctantly handing our phones over.

'Great, well, I shall say goodnight and trust you girls to

get a good night's sleep. Lights off in fifteen minutes – OK?'

'OKKKKKKAAAAAAY, sir.'

Two minutes after he leaves, we're all sitting on our beds and feeling a bit lost after being disconnected from the modern world, when Amber whips out her mobile phone and starts using it.

'What?! How have you still got your phone, Amber?' I asked.

'Yeh, I saw you hand it in,' said Ella, looking as confused as the rest of us.

'You saw me hand in *a phone*. I never said it was mine, did I?'

'Whose was it then?!' I said.

'It was one of my mum's old phones. I brought it with me as a decoy.'

'OMG – you are the smartest person I know!' shrieked Mia.

Amber looked very pleased with herself. I must hand it to her – it *was* a good plan and I wished I had thought of it too.

'Right, we have over eight hours until breakfast . . . Who wants to watch *Stranger Things* season four?'

I DO!!!!!!!!!!!

According to Mr Peters, it is now official lights-off time but we aren't planning on going to sleep any time soon. **HA HA HAAAAAAAAAAAAAAAAAAAAAAA!**

10.49 p.m.

There was a loud knock on the door. We all jumped out of our skins. Even though I'd seen the episodes before, it was much scarier watching it in a little wooden cabin that would be really easy for anyone to burst into.

'Who's going to get it?' I whispered.

Everyone started shaking their heads.

'What if it's a Demogorgon like in *Stranger Things*?' said Molly.

'What if it's Mr Peters coming to tell us off?!' said Mia.

'Oh, for goodness' sake! You're a bunch of babies!' said Amber, getting off her bed and throwing the door open. She stuck her head outside. 'There's no one there.'

How weird.

Feeling a bit creeped out now.

10.58 p.m.

I made Amber google 'Are Demogorgons real creatures?' . . . Apparently they're not. They are completely fictional. Phew.

11.12 p.m.

We've just had another loud knock on the door! This time, when I stuck my head out to look around, I saw Olive and Emmeline from the cabin next door doing exactly the same thing.

'Did someone knock on your door?' asked Emmeline.

'Yeh, we've had it twice now,' I replied.

'Same, I think there is a mystery ding-dong ditcher,' said Olive.

'Or maybe a mystery ding-dong Demogorgon!'

'What?!'

'Nothing.'

'Urgh! I hope they don't do it all night!'

'Me too!'

11.30 p.m.

After Knocks Four and Five, we were starting to get pretty annoyed. We were trying to enjoy watching *Stranger Things* and this ding-dong ditcher/Demogorgon was freaking us all out. We needed to go and speak to the teachers.

Me and Molly put on our onesies over our jammies and went to find Mr Peters. It didn't take long – he was sitting at the picnic tables, huddled together with Miss Moulson and the other teachers.

'Oh, erm, hello, girls. We're just enjoying a nice cup of, er . . .' said Mr Peters.

'CUP OF TEA!' finished Miss Moulson, giggling.

I don't know who they were trying to fool. We could clearly see a nearly empty bottle of wine on the table that they were *not so cleverly* trying to disguise by drinking it out of mugs.

'Sir, someone is running around ding-dong ditching the cabins and it keeps waking us up!' said Molly.

'Oh dear, girls. That does sound truly awful . . . but maybe just try to ignore it. They'll get bored eventually.'

'We've tried ignoring it, sir, but it's really loud!'

'Also, I'm a bit worried it could be a Demogorgon,' I said, which made Miss Moulson laugh even more.

Mr Peters sighed. 'OK, well, I promise we will patrol the area and make sure everyone is in their cabins and that there are no Demogorgons running wild in the woods just as soon as we have finished drinking our wi–'

'TEA!' finished Miss Moulson, almost spitting out her mouthful of wine in the process.

Fat lot of help they were being!

'Enjoy your TEA, sir,' we both said, walking off.

It's utter madness out there. The whole of Camp Firefly
is running riot and no one seems to care. We have now
had approximately 127 knocks on our door. I daren't look
outside as the boys are running around pantsing each
other – I'm afraid of what I might see. If you've not heard
of pantsing, it's when you pull someone's trousers down
for LOLs. Theo has tried to avoid this happening to
him by wearing three pairs of joggers at once, but I
fear it won't do him any good. In fact, I just heard
someone saying, 'HA HA, THEO – NICE RACING-
CAR BOXERS!' so I assume his plan has failed
miserably. Boys are SO immature . . . As a side note,
I can't believe Theo wears racing-car boxers!

Anyway, as it's way too noisy to sleep, we have decided to
take the **only logical approach** and stay up all night
instead. We're trying to decide what we should do to
keep us awake and so far the list is:

    * 12–1 a.m. – snacking and chatting

    * 1–2 a.m. – watch TikToks on Amber's phone

* 2–3 a.m. – rank top 100 hottest boys in the school

* 3–4 a.m. – more snacks

* 4–5 a.m. – cabin DISCO

* 5–6 a.m. – tell ghost stories

* 6–7 a.m. – free choice

* 7 a.m. – breakfast!

1.45 a.m.

Got bored so we pooled our sanitary-towel collection. Between us we had 74. Spent a long time discussing what to do with them. Ella wanted to construct a 3-D model of the Eiffel Tower, Amber and Molly wanted to make slippers, and Mia wanted to set fire to them! In the end, we decided the best (and safest) thing to do was stick them all on to one of us and then send that person out to haunt the camp – the added bonus was that hopefully it might help scare away the ding-dong ditcher too!

We're going to decide who goes by putting all our names in a hat and then picking one out . . . but we just realized we don't have a hat, so we're using Amber's bra (because she has the biggest cup size).

1.55 a.m.

I mean, if you had to guess who drew the short straw, who would you go with?

Yep. You got it! As if there was any doubt.

PS If this is my last-ever diary entry, you can assume that I had my head eaten off by a Demogorgon.

OMG, that was HILARIOUS. You should have heard the screaming!

I was knocking on cabin windows and then, when people looked out, I pressed my face right up to the window and sort of growled at them.

I felt like a superhero! Yes, OK . . . a superhero covered in sanitary towels, but a superhero nonetheless!

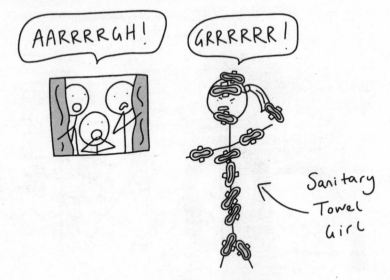

Then I heard a twig crack behind me – Mr Peters had come out to see what all the noise was. He shouted, 'Hey,

what's going on over there!' and started walking over
towards me.

I didn't want to get caught, as I knew I'd be in MASSIVE
trouble, so I decided to run towards the woods so that
I could hide. Unfortunately, the sanitary towels were
obscuring my vision and I ran face first into a tree – ouch!
The good thing was that the extra padding meant that I
didn't knock myself out or injure myself too badly.

I ducked behind the tree and waited. As the time
ticked slowly by, it was not lost on me how bonkers my
predicament actually was . . .

After a few more minutes, I dared to have a peek round the trunk. Luckily, Mr Peters must have got bored because the coast was clear. I took a deep breath and then ran as fast as I could back to our cabin.

The girls were all howling and I felt like a bit of a hero.

'You know, you'd make a great actress when you're older, Lottie,' said Amber.

'Really?'

'Yeh, I think you'd be especially well suited to a PERIOD drama.'

LOL!

I'm a little bit worried about getting into trouble tomorrow though, but fingers crossed the disguise will make it pretty difficult to identify me.

We have all sworn each other to secrecy!

3.05 a.m.

The late-night disco was a bit of a non-starter. We turned
the lights off, put some Harry Styles on Amber's phone
and used Ella's torch to make flashing lights. She had
to keep switching it off and on again though, so it got
boring after about forty-five seconds.

Turned out that no one had the energy to dance anyway.
Mia danced to 'As It Was' and then sat down again and
we all went back to watching TikToks.

5.59 a.m.

We've been eating sweets and watching TikToks for
almost three hours now and my eyes keep wanting to
close. Molly and Mia are already asleep, and Amber and
Ella look like they are about to drop off. I really wanted
to pull an all-nighter, but I think it was just a bit too . . .

TUESDAY 25 OCTOBER

There was a loud knock on the door, and I jumped right
out of my skin. It was pitch-black and I was convinced
it was the middle of the night. That's what getting forty-
five minutes of sleep does to you, I guess.

The knock turned out to be Mr Peters telling us that
we have twenty minutes to get ready for breakfast.
Somehow Amber managed to spring out of bed and into
the bathroom, and now she's been in the shower for
nearly ten minutes and no one else has time to have one.
Grrrrr!

I tried to move my legs, but I was so tired that they felt
like cement.

'Somebody help me! I'm about to die from lack of sleep!'
I said to no one in particular.

Molly appeared at the side of the bed, clutching a pack of

Tangfastics. She told me to open my mouth and then put five sweets inside it.

'This is the only way we're going to survive today,' she said with a wink – and she was right because about thirty seconds later I was twerking in the middle of the cabin in my pants!

THANK GOD FOR SUGAR!

I pulled on my clothes, sprayed myself all over with deodorant and dry shampoo, and gave myself a quick glance in the mirror. I look entirely AWFUL but who cares? I'm full of Tangfastics and I feel incredible!

7.08 a.m.

Oh, here comes Amber. She's finally out of the bathroom and she has a full face of make-up and is now blow-drying her hair. NO FAIR! She looks absolutely glowing – how does she do that when she was up until nearly 6 a.m.?!

Right, maybe I'll put on some mascara or something . . .

Actually, no time. We have to go – brekkie is in five minutes and I'm STARVING.

8.47 a.m.

Breakfast was really good. They had bacon, sausages, eggs and beans, so I loaded up my plate and had two slices of toast and orange juice too. Then I went for round two – because how often do you get a buffet breakfast?! I had a bowl of Cheerios and a bowl of fruit salad and then I had a strawberry yoghurt as well.

When I get home, I'm going to have a word with Mum about providing me with a more substantial breakfast before school . . . I don't think a bowl of boring cornflakes or a piece of toast cuts the mustard, TBH. Especially when she has to cut mouldy sections off the bread because she hasn't bothered to go shopping.

I mean, I don't want to be unfair – I'm not expecting a full-on buffet *every* day. I'm just saying that tropical fruit salad, pastries, a bacon bap, homemade waffles and a selection of freshly squeezed juices would probably set me up better for the day, that's all.

Anyway, there was one big topic of convo around the canteen this morn: **THE HAUNTING OF CAMP FIREFLY!**

Apparently several cabins reported seeing a ghost/ mummy/zombie wandering around outside in the middle of the night. A few people were really upset recalling how they'd heard knocking on the windows and their cabin doors and they'd opened the curtains to see an 'angry white apparition'.

I know it's mean but me and everyone from our cabin were all trying REALLY hard not to laugh!

Mr Peters tried to calm everyone down and tell them that there is no such thing as ghosts/mummies/zombies so it would have only been someone playing a practical joke. He also told us to . . .

We all went 'OOOOOOOOOOOOOOOOOOH!'

Theo put his hand up and said, 'What will the consequences be, sir?'

'Trust me, Theo – you don't want to find out!'

Molly nudged me. 'That basically means he doesn't know.'

Amber agreed and said we shouldn't take his vague threats very seriously – she's already trying to convince me to haunt the camp again after lights out! We've saved all the sanitary towels, so hopefully they will still be sticky enough and I must admit I kinda liked being Sanitary Towel Girl. It was fun!

After breakfast we were stuffed, so we headed back to our cabin and managed to sneak in a thirty-minute snooze before we had to meet on the basketball court and find out what we'll be doing.

What a day. I've barely had time to breathe. Well, actually that's a stupid thing to say because if I didn't

have time to breathe I'd be dead, and also breathing
is controlled by the automatic nervous system, so you
don't even have to think about it. Unless you start
thinking about it . . . and now I can't stop thinking about
breathing and I'm breathing too deeply and I must sound
weird because Amber just went: 'Lottie, why do you
sound like Darth Vader?'

Anyway, let me get back to the day. So we made our way
over to the basketball court and Mr Peters told us to
gather round so he could make some announcements.

'Morning, campers! I hope you're all looking forward
to the first day of camp and the wonderful things we
have planned for you. To kick things off, I have a few
announcements. As well as the activities we have
planned, on Wednesday evening we will be holding a
camp concert. I want you and your
teams to put on a show for us. This
could be anything at all – acting,
singing, dancing, poetry! What we
want to see is you all working together
to do something brilliant to try to win
the Camp Firefly Cup!'

There was an audible gasp from the drama nerds and a groan from the sporty types, who hate stuff like that. I was kind of excited about it – it sounded cool.

'And Miss Moulson and I discussed last night that it would be a fun idea to pair each cabin from Kingswood High with a cabin from Willow Park College. You will be doing all your activities AND your performance for the concert together, so you should get to know each other pretty well!'

Oh God. I bet they decided that while they were drinking their 'TEA'!

Amber nudged me. 'That is NOT a fun idea!'

'I know, it's about the third least fun idea I've heard this year.'

'What were the first and second least fun ideas?'

'When the Fun Police introduced Screen-Free Sundays and when Toby offered to catch my farts in jam jars and sell them on eBay.'

'OMG, your family are weird.'

'I know . . .'

'OK, so without further ado,' Mr Peters continued, 'I'm sure you're all desperate to find out who you've been paired with from the other school. Miss Moulson, would you like to announce the teams?'

I'm not sure that 'desperate' was the right word – 'dreading' would have been more like it. I just had the most overwhelming feeling that my bad luck was going to continue.

Miss Moulson called out two cabin names at a time and gradually the big group began to get smaller as the paired-off cabins went off with their group leaders to their activities. I noticed that Daniel and Theo looked delighted to be paired with a group of smiley, fun-looking girls, and Jess, Isha and Poppy seemed to get a friendly group too.

Soon there were only four cabins left, including ours and Pointy Nose's. We had a fifty-fifty chance of it going our way.

'Please don't let it be Pointy Nose, please don't let it be Pointy Nose, please don't let it be Pointy Nose', I muttered under my breath.

'Right, so on to Shooting Stars . . . Who shall we pair you girls with . . . ? Aha, yes, of course! I think you girls would have a brilliant time with the Mossy Bottom cabin, which houses one of my star pupils and head girl, Phoebe Higglesworth.'

I got this really strong sinking feeling in my stomach and I didn't want to look up.

'Let me guess . . . Phoebe Higglesworth has got to be Pointy Nose, right?' I whispered to Ella who was standing next to me.

She sighed. 'Unfortunately, you guessed right.'

The Mossy Bottom girls didn't look any more pleased about it than we did. In fact, as they came over to join us, they looked at us as if we were something they'd just scraped off their shoes. I suppose they'd been hoping to be paired with a boys' cabin and I don't blame them really.

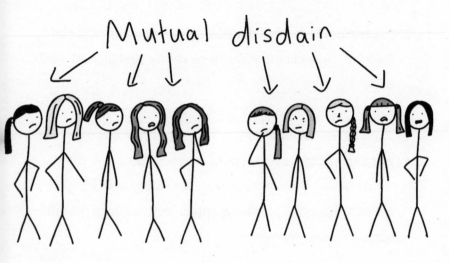

We all stood there, not speaking, until Kai came over to us, clapped his hands together and started handing out schedules.

Pointy Nose and her crew immediately came to life. **'Hiiiiiiii, Kaiiiiii,'** they all chimed, giggling.

Amber sighed and rolled her eyes – like we hadn't all had the exact same reaction to him yesterday.

I looked down at my timetable. It sounded full-on! We have raft building, a sensory trail, fencing, abseiling and loads more. In retrospect, maybe it would have been a good idea to get more than forty-five minutes of sleep . . .

'Right, first things first,' said Kai. 'We need a group name – it can be as wild or wacky as you like . . . Any ideas?'

'Oh, I do! How about Whizzy Weirdos?' shouted Molly.

'Or the Cool Cats!' suggested Mia.

'Or the . . . Slightly . . .' I began. 'Awkward . . .' *Oh God – where was I going with this?!* '. . . Potatoes?'

Amber stared at me, agog . . .

Stupid, stupid mouth!!

Phoebe and her crew all started laughing hysterically.

'Oh, wow – you guys are SO CRINGE!' she said.

Kai, clearly trying to be diplomatic, said, 'Do you have any better ideas, Phoebe?'

She folded her arms and said, 'Well, yes, actually, I do . . . ummm . . . I need a moment to –'

'Right,' said Kai. 'Well, we're running out of time so we'll just have to pick from those already suggested. Because it's original and made me laugh, let's go with the Slightly Awkward Potatoes.'

'What?! I'm NOT slightly awkward and I'm definitely NOT a potato!' shrieked Phoebe.

'You are now!' said Kai with a wink.

Phoebe gritted her teeth. 'We can't have a name like that! It makes us sound like a joke!'

Kai completely ignored her. 'So, Slightly Awkward

Potatoes – follow me! We don't want to be late!'

'Okaaaaaay, Kaiiiiii,' chimed Amber, practically running after him.

Our first activity was the **SENSORY TRAIL**. Kai led us to the start of the course and we saw another team waiting to begin. As we got closer, I realized it was Daniel and his group and I felt really weird – sort of a mixture of excitement and dread because things are still a little bit awks between us.

The WPC girls, on the other hand, were super excited. I guess going to an all-girls school they don't get much exposure to boys, because as soon as they saw the boys they started nudging each other excitedly and chatting about which one was the hottest. The worst part was when I heard Phoebe declare that she liked Daniel. I know I had no right to be jealous . . . but I couldn't help it.

Molly must have heard her comment too, because she spun round and said, 'Well, you can't *like* Daniel because he's not available.'

Phoebe goes, 'Oh really . . . why not?'

Then Amber says SUPER loudly so that EVERYONE could hear: 'Because he's Lottie's sort of boyfriend.'

Phoebe scoffed and turned to me. '*Sort of boyfriend?* What does that even mean? He's either your boyfriend or he isn't – which is it?'

OMG, I hated being put on the spot like that and I hated even more that it was Amber putting me on it. It was a bit like when you are playing Twister and you already have your hands and feet on different colours and then someone spins and you have to put your leg on the opposite side of the board. Basically, it's almost impossible to do without making a complete fool of yourself! Or dislocating your kneecap.

So everyone was staring at me and waiting for an answer, and I didn't want to say yes because that would be untrue, and I also didn't want to say no because I didn't really want Pointy Nose to think that Daniel was single either.

I had no choice though. He wasn't mine and he could do what he wanted – so, in an attempt to sound really unbothered about the whole thing, I said, 'Nah, he's not my boyfriend and you are very welcome to him.'

Molly did a big cough and it was only then that I noticed Daniel crouching right behind me, tying his shoelace. I caught his eye and, although he was attempting to look busy finishing his laces, I could tell that he had heard everything.

'Right! Is everybody ready?' shouted Kai. I was grateful for the interruption, TBH.

'I'm ready, Kai,' said Amber in the stupidest voice I had ever heard. It was all high and cutesy like a four-year-old's.

'Why are you speaking like that?' I asked her.

'Like what?' she said in her normal voice.

I rolled my eyes. 'When you speak to Kai, you put on this weird baby voice.'

'I SO DO NOT!'

'Girls, please,' said Kai. 'We need to get started.'

Amber's cheeks flushed red – I could tell she was embarrassed that he had called us out.

'Right,' he continued, clapping his hands together. 'Blindfolds!'

We each took one out of a big box. They were actually a bit more like scuba-diving masks and they made everything completely black so you couldn't cheat at all.

Next, he put us all in a big, long line and we had to put one hand on the shoulder of the person in front and then the other on a rope that would lead us round the course. The fun part was that he completely mixed up the different groups, so we had no idea who was in front of or behind us.

Then we started the trail by moving forward slowly. If you came across a sticky-out bit of tree or an uneven bit of ground, you were meant to pass the message backwards through the chain to help the others out. There were also proper obstacles like tunnels, bridges, mazes and stepping stones.

It was totally surreal not being able to see. I think we take our sight for granted and it was cool using our other senses, like hearing and touch, to help us figure out where we were. I quickly worked out that Phoebe was the person in front of me as she was complaining about everything and saying stuff like **'EWWWWW!** I think my trainers are getting mud on them' and **'OMG**, nature is so **GROSS!'**

The person behind me was being super quiet and although I kept shouting things out like **'WATCH OUT! A BRANCH IS ABOUT TO HIT YOU IN THE FACE!'** they didn't really say much back apart from a few 'Mmmmms' and 'Thanks' every so often. Oh, and when a branch actually did hit them in the face: 'OW!' I had warned them though, so it wasn't really my fault! I did think it was a boy because I could tell they were taller than me and their voice sounded deeper . . . I just couldn't work out who it was.

Right at the end of the course we had to separate ourselves from the chain to crawl under a big army-style net. It was very hard not being able to see, as we had no idea how long it would go on for. I got totally confused and started crawling in the wrong direction. That's when I somehow kicked the person behind me right in the face and when they shouted, 'OWWWW – THAT'S MY NOSE!' I had a sinking feeling that their voice was a bit more familiar than I had first thought.

Amber and Molly had already finished, and they helped me out of the net. When I took my blindfold off, I saw Daniel on the ground clutching his nose and a pool of blood collecting on the mud.

'What?!' I said.

'I think he means it's OK, he's fine,' said Theo, as he crouched on the ground, handing Daniel tissues to try to stop the blood.

Kai came over and took a look at Daniel's nose to assess the damage. 'Hmmm, I think it might be best for you to get checked in the medical room, Daniel. Would anyone like to volunteer to take him over?'

Phoebe jumped up like someone had just put a cockroach in her knickers. **'OHH, MEEEE, I WOULD!'**

'OK, Phoebe, that's very helpful. Thank you.'

'No worries at all, Kai,' she said, smiling sweetly before putting her arm round Daniel and walking him proudly away.

I grumbled to Amber. 'She looks as smug as my mum did when she won a handheld vacuum cleaner in the raffle at my primary school's summer fair.'

Amber, annoyed on my behalf, and probably also jealous of Phoebe for getting into Kai's good books, decided to shout out after them both . . .

'AND just so you know, Phoebe . . . HE'S NOT A BLIMMIN' HANDHELD VACUUM CLEANER!'

Why, oh why, do I tell things to Amber?!!

I put my hand on my left shoulder and it still felt warm. Daniel's hand had been there for half an hour and I didn't even know it.

Lunch was hot dogs and potato wedges, which were pretty good, but I was too mortified by what happened at the sensory trail to eat much. At least I got to catch up with Jess though. When she plonked her tray down next to mine, she immediately clocked something was up.

'Oh no, what's wrong?' she asked.

'Well, you know how things are a bit weird with Daniel?'

'Yeh . . . did you sort stuff out?'

'Not . . . exactly.'

'What do you mean by *not exactly?*'

'I mean . . . I kicked him in the face, gave him a nosebleed and compared him to a handheld vacuum cleaner.'

'WHAT?!?' she said, almost choking on a piece of hot dog.

'That's not strictly speaking true, Lottie,' interrupted Amber. 'I actually helped explain that he WASN'T a handheld vacuum cleaner.'

'Well, that's OK then, I guess!' said Jess.

'Exactly,' said Amber.

I didn't really agree with them, but I was keen to change the subject, so I asked Jess how she was getting on with her WPC group and she said they were all really nice. They've already agreed to do a comedy sketch for the concert, and she's really excited about it. I wish things could be so easy for us. Hmph.

Amber spent the rest of the break going ON and ON about how unfair it was that Phoebe volunteered to help Daniel before anyone else had a chance, and how that meant that Kai probably liked her best now. Then she bombarded us with increasingly bonkers questions . . .

Did we think Kai was good-looking? Yes.

Did we think he liked her? Yes, as a friend.

Did we think if she was older, he would like her as more than a friend? We said, 'No idea,' even though I thought it was unlikely.

Should she come back to Camp Firefly when she's eighteen and ask him out? FIRM NO!

After the Kai interrogation, we began to get SERIOUSLY tired, so it was time to dose up on more Tangfastics before our next activity: **THE BIG SWING**.

It looked super high, so I was a bit nervous about doing it. By that point, however, the tiredness was taking over, so I just saw it as an opportunity to sit down. I went on with Molly and it actually turned out to be really relaxing – so much so that I actually fell asleep on it.

Apparently it was pretty fun if you were conscious, but I did feel better after my power nap, so whatevs.

I was really looking forward to having some free time after dinner, to catch up with Poppy, Jess and Isha, but Mr Peters informed us that the evening's social time was cancelled so that we could get together with our groups and decide what we would be doing for the camp concert.

GROAN!!

I can't think of anything I'd rather do less than hang out with Phoebe and her WPC gang – I think I'd rather go to bed early. In fact, I know I'd rather go to bed early. *In fact,* I could probably curl up and fall asleep on the cold, hard ground of the basketball court.

10.02 p.m.

Well, that was awful. They absolutely hate us and TBH the feeling is mutual.

We were meant to come to an agreement of what we would be performing but it was going absolutely nowhere. We had a brainstorm to discuss our ideas – I thought we had some really great ones . . .

Ella: Taylor Swift medley.

Amber: Catwalk show. (TBF she has got about a hundred outfits with her.)

Molly: Top five TikTok dances of the year.

Mia: Gymnastics demonstration (but can only really do cartwheels and forward rolls).

Me: A play about a toaster that wants to be human.

Phoebe said, 'OMG! First you call our team the Slightly Awkward Potatoes and now you want us to do a play about toasters. I'm seriously worried there is something wrong with you!'

I looked around at my friends, hoping they'd have my back, but to my horror they just shrugged their shoulders as if they agreed with her! I mean, yeh, I'll admit that maybe mine was a bit 'out there' but it's not like she had any better ideas.

I said, 'Well, at least I'm trying! You've not suggested anything.'

'Well, actually, I do have an idea. I think we should do an interpretive dance about climate change. It's one that me and the girls already know – we've performed it as part of a school concert before and it was REALLY impactful. A lot of parents in the audience were crying at the end.'

It sounded about as dull as listening to Toby talk about *Minecraft*!

We were all arguing about it when Miss Moulson came over and said that the other groups had already made a decision and that we needed to decide soon so that we could get on with our rehearsals. She said that the only fair way to agree was to hold a vote – so we did . . . but stupidly no one voted for my HIGHLY ORIGINAL idea except me, so we were stuck doing the highly unoriginal climate change dance. Amber said it was all our fault as we should have been more strategic about it, instead of just shouting out ideas like impatient toddlers.

The worst thing was that there were only six dancing parts in the performance, so when it came to agreeing who would do what, we put all our hands up to dance. Phoebe said, 'Miss Moulson, as we haven't got much time and we already know the parts really well, don't you think it makes more sense for the Willow Park College students to do the dancing?'

Me and my friends looked at Miss Moulson in outrage. Surely she wouldn't agree to this!

But what she actually said was, 'Yes, that sounds very sensible – thanks, Phoebe.'

'You're welcome, miss,' said Phoebe. 'Just thinking of making things as smooth as possible for the Kingswood High students.'

'Well, it's wonderful to see you being so considerate of your team!' replied Miss Moulson.

The WPC girls all sat there looking super smug.

HOW UNFAIR WAS THAT?!

Amber put her hands on her hips and huffed, 'What are we meant to do then, miss?!'

She was only saying what we were all thinking!

'Don't worry – I have the perfect idea! I'll be back in a minute,' said Miss Moulson, walking off.

'You should be thanking us,' said Phoebe, smirking. 'We've just saved you from making fools of yourselves on stage.'

'Says who?! We could be EXCELLENT dancers for all you know!' said Molly, also putting her hands on her hips.

Phoebe laughed. 'Well, are you?!'

'Ummm,' replied Molly. 'I'm OK . . . Amber is all right . . . Lottie is . . . hmm, well not so much –'

Why do my friends keep throwing me under a bus?!

'Hey, that's a bit unfair actually, Molly,' I told her. 'I played a very good dancing crab in the spring musical, remember!'

The WPC girls lost it at this point, and I felt rather cross with Molly for somehow managing to make me embarrass myself (again).

'Anyway,' Molly continued, 'the point is that you shouldn't simply *assume* you're better than us. It's very arrogant!'

'We aren't assuming anything,' said Phoebe. 'It's an opinion we've formed based on the behaviour you have

demonstrated in the short time that we've known
you . . . You all just seem, how shall we say this . . .
quite immature?'

Amber got really annoyed at that. 'Immature?! How dare
you! What have we done that's immature?'

'Well, what about that, for example . . .' And Phoebe
pointed to Ella and Mia, behind me.

Oh. Maybe she did have a point.

'Here we go . . .' Miss Moulson had come back, clutching

a brown box. She set it down on the floor and clapped her hands together. 'Percussion! This will really bring the performance to life – don't you think, girls?'

Then she walked off to ruin somebody else's day. Amber was absolutely fuming.

I was NOT put on this earth to PLAY PERCUSSION!!!

TBF, I'd never imagined her playing a harmonica either.

Still, if percussion was what we had to do, then I wanted to get something good! I guess we all had the same idea as everyone made a dash for the box at the same time. It felt like being three years old again and scrambling to get the best set of maracas at Sing and Sign. Sadly, I wasn't quick enough off the mark and ended up with the triangle. Rubbish.

Next, it was time to rehearse the performance and arrange the percussion to it. I didn't really get how the dance was about climate change when it basically just involved them prancing around dramatically and looking sad, but, as much as I hate to admit it, the WPC girls were pretty good. As the triangle player though, it was decided that I only needed to hit it three times in the entire five-minute performance, so I was pretty much a spare wheel.

I think all the Shooting Stars girls felt the same, which was a shame, as it could have been really fun performing in the concert, but instead everything felt a bit flat and now I am not looking forward to it AT ALL.

10.35 p.m.

EEEK. We had totally forgotten about the room inspection and when Mr Peters came round to make sure our room was in order . . . it um . . . wasn't.

'What on earth has been going on in here?' he said, seeing the mess as soon as he stepped through the door.

Molly said, 'Amber got her period, sir,' like that was a good explanation for having the entire floor covered in sanitary towels.

Luckily, he didn't question us any further, but he only scored us 3/10. HMPH.

He also handed out a stack of postcards and said that we should write to our parents, and he would post them for us tomorrow morning.

'What are we meant to say, sir? We've only been here a day!' said Amber.

'Whatever you like – I'm sure they would just like to know you are alive and well and that they don't have to worry about you!'

Wrote my postcard to send to the Fun Police.

Dear Mum and Dad,

Good news – I'm not dead!

I had a nice time today . . . except for all the blood.
I have a gig as a triangle player and I fell asleep
ten metres in the air.

Last night I went haunting the woods at 2 a.m.
and only got forty-five minutes' sleep, so I'm
surviving on Haribo. Please can you post me
some more Tangfastics?

Love,

Lottie xx

PS The teachers all drink wine out of mugs and
pretend it's tea!

Hopefully that will be reassuring for them.

We had planned that I would go out haunting again tonight, but by the time they had stuck all the sanitary towels back on me I had fallen asleep standing up. I've never thought it was possible to fall asleep standing up, but apparently it is! It was quite weird (especially when you're covered in sanitary towels).

Anyway, we decided that maybe we should leave the haunting for tonight and get some much-needed shut-eye, so I'm off to bed and I feel like I could sleep for a gazillion years.

WEDNESDAY 26 OCTOBER

I had a restless night and a terrible dream. I was being chased by a crowd of angry triangles, handheld vacuum cleaners and Always Ultra with wings.

I woke up screaming (and still covered in sanitary towels).

Everyone was very annoyed because it was only 6 a.m. Maybe the three bags of Tangfastics I had yesterday were a little bit OTT – oops.

8.35 a.m.

I could kill my so-called 'friends'.

On the walk to breakfast everyone kept looking at me and then whispering and giggling. I checked myself over . . . Had I grown a really long, thick chin hair overnight? Had I forgotten to put trousers on? Maybe I'd accidentally put a pair of pants on my head? I ran my hands over my head and body, but everything seemed to be in order.

When we got into the canteen, it got even worse – people were nudging each other, pointing and shrieking with laughter.

'What's wrong? Do I look OK?' I asked the girls, but Molly just shrugged, and Amber said I was 'being paranoid'.

I sighed, sat down and started tucking into my bacon sarnie.

'Oh, poor Lottie, did you get your period?'

Urgh. It was Pointy Nose and her crew, sniggering behind me.

I spun round and looked at her blankly.

'Maybe you've not used them before, but I only wanted to make sure you knew that sanitary towels aren't much use when they are on your back . . .'

What was she on about?!

I put my hand on the back of my T-shirt and groaned. Then, as the tables surrounding us burst out laughing, I flushed bright red. There was a sanitary towel stuck to my top.

I pulled it off and screwed it up into a ball.

'I'm not an idiot. I've used them loads of times before!'
I said.

I wish I'd kept my mouth shut as that made everyone laugh even more.

I put my sandwich down and lowered my head. I wasn't hungry any more.

'Why didn't you tell me I had that thing stuck on my back?' I whispered to Molly and Amber, when PN and her crew finally walked off.

'I was going to – I just . . .' Molly trailed off. 'We thought it would be funny, I guess.'

'It wasn't very funny for me!'

'No. I know. I'm really sorry, Lottie,' said Molly sheepishly.

'Oh, chill out, Lottie. It's no big deal,' huffed Amber. 'We were only having a laugh. You don't have to take everything so seriously.'

I sighed. Yeh, no big deal, because it happened to me and not her. This would never have happened if I was in a cabin with Jess – there is no way she'd have let me walk into the canteen like that. Everything would have been so much better if we hadn't been split up.

On the way back to the cabins after breakfast I saw her sitting on a picnic table with Isha, and they had a pack of chocolate digestives in front of them. Jess took two out of the packet and handed one to Isha, then they both put them on their foreheads, laughing.

My heart sank. They were playing the Biscuit Face Challenge.

I was beginning to seriously hate Angela. She knew exactly which insecurities to tap into.

'Right, come on, guys,' said Ella, interrupting my thoughts. 'We've got raft building now and Kai says we need to put on old clothes that we don't mind getting wet.'

'Old clothes?!' said Amber, screwing up her nose. 'What are they? I didn't bring anything like that.'

Honestly, living with Amber 24/7 is hard work!

2.04 p.m.

We ended up being late for raft building because, while the rest of us pulled on joggers and old T-shirts, Amber spent half an hour curling her hair and complaining that she didn't want ANY of her clothing getting ruined (despite being told that we should only bring clothing we didn't mind getting ruined). After we'd had to endure a catwalk show with about ten different outfit choices, she decided on sequin leggings and a hot-pink vest top.

Kai said he'd 'never seen anyone dress up so much for raft building before' but I guess he's never met anyone like Amber. She is one of a kind – I'll give her that!

She batted her eyelashes at him and put on her cutesy annoying voice again. 'What, these old clothes, Kai? They were just the first things I pulled out of my suitcase.'

I rolled my eyes at Molly and she laughed.

'Right, well, anyway . . .' boomed Kai, clearly keen to get on with things. 'Everyone grab a life jacket and helmet.'

Amber looked horrified. 'But what about my hair? I've just curled it, and I don't want to get helmet hair!'

'Oh, for goodness' sake!' I said, grabbing a helmet and shoving it towards her. 'Just put the blimmin' thing on!'

'Jeez, all right!' she huffed. 'Are you sure you don't have PMT, Lottie?!'

Luckily for her, Kai interrupted us: 'Right, everyone. Let's get started!'

He explained that each group would be building a raft out of six large plastic barrels, two metal poles and a bunch of rope. I had to admit it looked pretty impossible, but he promised he'd help make it secure.

We set to work. We had to roll the barrels together and then tie them really tight using special knots that were pretty complicated to get right. Then we had to slide poles under the rope and roll them around to the sides of the barrels to help hold everything together. That was it – our raft was done! It was quite simple really but, looking at it, I was a bit sceptical that it would stay together once we all got on it.

We were each given an oar to use for rowing and Kai helped us launch it into the water. I say 'water', but it was a murky green opaque colour, which looked incredibly uninviting and cold.

'Come on, guys,' said Molly, who was already at the back of the raft to make room for everyone else.

Amber was next, despite initially refusing to get in for fear of getting her hair wet – but seeing Kai at the edge of the water offering his hand out to help her was too much of a temptation. She made a particular show of nearly falling off. (I think it was only so that she could grab on to him.)

I watched as everyone else got on. Mia was wobbling about all over the place, and Ella nearly fell in. I wasn't really sure I wanted to get on the raft after all.

'Ummmm, I think maybe I'll pass,' I said. 'I mean, there could be anything in there . . . Toads, eels, even crocs!'

'Crocs?! Honestly. Where do you think we are . . . Africa?!'

I spun round to see Phoebe and the WPC girls laughing and smirking at me. They were all perfectly balanced on their raft, making it look simple. Right, I wasn't going to let Pointy Nose have the satisfaction of seeing me too scared to do this! Kai held the raft steady, and I clambered on, trying to look as confident as I could. It was super wobbly though and I couldn't help shrieking.

Once everyone was on their rafts, Kai clapped his hands together and said, 'Right, well, your rafts look absolutely brilliant. In fact, they look so sturdy I was thinking we could have a race. One side of the lake to the other – what do you think?'

Everyone else cheered, **'YAY!!!!!'**

I said 'Yay' out loud, but internally I said, *Oh, bum*, because I was not convinced that our raft could make it across the lake without falling apart.

'OK. On your marks, get set, GO!'

We started paddling as fast as we could, but while the other rafts moved forward, ours kept spinning round in circles. No matter how hard we tried, we were making very little progress. No one was working as a team, and it was a complete mess.

I looked ahead, frustrated. Theo and Daniel's raft was nearly halfway across the lake, closely followed by Phoebe's raft, and even Jess and Poppy had made a decent start and were over a quarter of the way there.

I felt a strong burst of competitive energy pulse through me – we needed to beat Pointy Nose and Team Mean!

'WE NEED TO PADDLE FASTER!' I roared.

'Aye aye, captain!' said Mia with a salute.

Molly took control and started counting out when we should put our paddles in the water, so eventually we were all doing it in unison.

It was working – we were making progress at last. And we were fast!

It wasn't long before we overtook Jess and Poppy and we were right behind Phoebe.

'Come on, Shooting Stars – we can do it!' shouted Amber.

I smiled at her; I was pleased that she had got into the task. She's so much more fun when she drops the attitude and lets her guard down.

With a few more strokes, we were neck and neck with

the WPC girls, and Phoebe looked horrified. That's when she took her oar and started jabbing it into our barrels, trying to push us backwards.

'Hey, that's not fair!' cried Mia. 'You're cheating!'

'*Hey, that's not fair!*' mimicked Phoebe.

'Come on, guys! Paddle!' I shouted.

We were just about to gain the lead when I felt an oar thwack into the back of my life vest. It threw me completely off balance and the next thing I knew I was sliding off my barrel and falling head first into the murky water.

SPLASH! I came up spluttering and choking.

'Ooooops!' said Phoebe. 'I don't know what happened there . . . I think my oar must have slipped.'

My friends were shouting to see if I was OK and trying to offer me their oars to hold on to, but there was no way I was going to be able to get back on the raft, so the only option was to swim to the other side of the lake too.

It was absolutely terrifying! I couldn't stop imagining horrible things lurking in the murky water, even though I knew I was being ridiculous because there is no such thing as swamp monsters.

When I got there, Daniel had already made it across and had got off his raft, so he offered me a hand and helped me up on to the jetty.

'Are you OK, Lottie?' he asked.

I didn't want to look at him in case I cried (also I obvs looked like a drowned rat).

I picked a bit of pond weed off my chin. 'Yes. Yeh. I think so . . . thank you,' I managed to say.

Kai came over to check I was OK too, just as the WPC girls' raft arrived, closely followed by the Shooting Stars raft.

'I hope you didn't push Lottie off on purpose, Phoebe,' said Kai.

'WHAT?! NO! Of course not.' She looked at him with puppy-dog eyes. 'I would never do that, Kaiiiiiiii.'

'Oh my life . . . How pathetic are they?' whispered Amber. 'Flirting with the poor guy when he's just trying to get on with his job.'

I remembered my mum telling me about the phrase 'pot calling the kettle black', but I didn't think pointing it out to Amber would really help matters.

Phoebe then turned to me. 'Oh, Lottie, you poor thing, you look an absolute mess. Would you like us to take you back to your cabin to get dry?'

She is SO FAKE!!

'Don't worry! We'll take her!' said Molly, steering me
away from them.

When we got back to the cabin, I had a lovely hot shower
and put on clean, dry clothes and they had never felt so
good.

3.25 p.m.

After lunch, we had fencing. We got to poke swords
at the WPC girls, which I think we all found quite
therapeutic – especially after the stunt Phoebe pulled
today. I don't care what she said – it was a hundred per
cent on purpose.

Now we're in the middle of dress rehearsals for tonight's
concert and I'm writing in my diary because, apart from
the odd bash, blow or ping of percussion, none of us
Shooting Stars have very much to do.

We're all dressed head to toe in black because
apparently that makes us look sophisticated and arty.

Personally, I think it just made us look and feel even more miserable.

The saddest percussion band you've ever seen...

So, while PN and the WPC girls prance around and practise, we are sitting at the side, chatting. Or, if you want to be more specific, I'm writing in my diary and listening to the others chat . . . or, if you want to be even more specific, we are all listening to Amber chat about how HOT Kai is and how one day she'd like to marry him!

I just pointed out (again) that he was much too old for her and by the time she was old enough to get married he'd have probably left Camp Firefly and moved back to Australia. Then she looked so sad I thought she was about to burst out crying.

Luckily, Molly distracted her by shouting, 'Not being rude or anything, but what has the dance got to do with climate change?'

Phoebe gave her a snooty reply: 'If you need to have art explained to you, then you can't be very well cultured!'

Amber said, 'How dare you! I've been to the Loo in Paris AND I've seen the *Moaning Lisa*!'

'It's the "Louvre" and it's the "*Mona Lisa*",' said Phoebe, shaking her head.

'Whatever!'

The rest of the session largely involved them all getting really cross with us for not timing the percussion correctly to the dance, but if the dance was less boring, then maybe we'd do a better job . . .

ABSOLUTELY FUMING/MORTIFYINGLY EMBARRASSED/NEVER GOING TO BE ABLE TO FACE PEOPLE AGAIN.

After dinner, I got back to the cabin to get ready for the concert and realized that my diary was missing. I looked everywhere: under the beds, in the cupboards, in the suitcases – and nothing! I was starting to panic because this is all pretty personal, y'know, and I couldn't bear the thought of anyone else reading it. Then I started to get angry at myself. Why did I even bring it with me?! What a stupid idea!

The last place I remembered having it was at the concert rehearsals. Maybe someone had found it and handed it in? I decided to go and ask Kai where the lost property was.

I came out of our cabin and started to walk over to the main building and that's when I saw Pointy Nose standing on a picnic bench surrounded by a large group. She looked as if she was telling a funny sort of joke because everyone was laughing and giggling at her.

I moved a bit closer, keen to find out what was making everyone laugh so much. As I got nearer, I could hear what she was saying and it sounded kinda familiar. I got an uneasy feeling in my tummy, then I squinted and looked closer to see what was in her hands . . . It couldn't be . . . could it?

It was.

It was **MY DIARY** and Phoebe was reading out my private thoughts and feelings to **EVERYONE**.

'Oh my god, guys, you have to hear this bit!' She was laughing so hard that she was finding it difficult to even read.

Another ripple of laughter rose from the crowd, and I cringed. *This can't be happening, can it?* I thought to myself. *Surely this is just a bad dream!* But Phoebe hadn't finished there . . .

'*Saturday, twenty-second of October. We also bought a box of tampons and a pack of sanitary towels – my periods seem to be kind of regular now so I don't think I'll get one at camp, but I also don't want to get caught short, as Mum would say.*'

I wanted to die of shame. That's when I noticed Daniel. Like me, he had come out of his cabin to find out what was going on and he had heard every single word.

'**OOOH**, this bit is interesting . . . *Sunday, eleventh of September. I know that me and Daniel aren't a thing any more, but I still get all nervous when I see him – does that mean I like him?! He's been looking especially cute lately . . .* **HAAAA! OMG**, this is so pathetic!'

I felt my eyes fill with tears; I didn't know what to do. I wanted to get my diary back and stop her, but I also wanted to run away and hide.

People started to whisper and point at me. I felt so hopeless, standing there on my own.

Then I saw Amber stride through the crowd and grab the diary from Phoebe's hands.

'I'll take that!' she said really loudly. 'You have no right taking other people's property! And you have no right laughing at Lottie like that!'

I couldn't love Amber any more in that minute!

But she didn't stop there . . .

'So what if she brings tampons and sanitary towels on school trips? There is nothing shameful about getting your period, is there? And so what if she has a crush on Daniel? She's allowed to have crushes, you know . . .'

GO, AMBER!

'. . . OK it might be bordering on a little bit obsessive and maybe she could stop going on about him 24/7 as it does get quite boring . . . but that's just Lottie!'

Ummm, bit harsh?!

'. . . And Lottie does not have to apologize for being herself, OK? I mean, yes, she might have boring hair and weird, skinny bird legs . . .'

Right, I think that's enough now, Amber!

'. . . and, yes, she might never grow out of her A-cup bra . . . And, yes, she does sometimes say some MEGA-CRINGE and quite frankly BONKERS stuff, but –'

'OK, AMBER, I THINK EVERYONE GETS THE MESSAGE NOW!' shouted Jess.

'BUT despite all those things . . . we love her just the way she is!' finished Amber. 'And if anyone is **immature** and **pathetic** around here, it's certainly not Lottie – **it's you!**'

PN just stood there, open-mouthed and totally lost for words.

'ROASTED!' I heard one of the boys shout before the crowd began to drift away.

Amber came running over to me, put her arm round me and led me back to the cabin. I don't think I've ever felt so grateful to have her as a friend.

'I guess it's OK for me to be a bit of a cow to you,' she explained, 'but, if anyone else does it, then they are toast – that's just how our friendship works, OK?'

I laughed. 'OK . . . I really don't know how I'm going to live this down though. So many people heard her . . . I'm shuddering every time I think about it.'

Amber gave me a hug. 'Oh, come on . . . it wasn't that bad. I mean, wow – so people know you've got unicorn name labels in your underwear and that you still have a thing for Daniel? Big deal. I mean, it's hardly front-page news, is it?'

I smiled. 'I guess not.'

Sometimes having Amber on your side feels like a really good thing.

I am absolutely dreading the concert though. Not only do I have to get up on stage and have the whole camp look at me and whisper about me, I also have to do it with Phoebe who is just about the meanest person I've ever met!

9.46 p.m.

Feeling so much better about everything!

Despite me dreading it, the concert was actually pretty fun. Jess, Poppy and Isha's group did a comedy sketch making fun of the teachers and it was hilarious. Daniel and Theo's group did football tricks and keepy-uppies, and there were singers, dancers, gymnastics, bands and more. I thought it was all great, apart from the fact that I knew we had to get up there and do our act too, and the worst thing was that we were on last.

I watched the other groups with an increasing feeling of dread, so it was hard to properly enjoy the other acts. Even though I only had to hit my triangle three times, I just REALLY didn't want to get up on stage with that traitor Phoebe.

Finally, it was our turn. Kai climbed the stairs to the stage and announced us: 'And now for an interpretive dance called "Our Climate" from the Slightly Awkward Potatoes!'

The audience laughed and the WPC girls gave me evil eyes. I started to feel really annoyed with them. I mean, yeh, it's a bit of a silly name but get over it! Why do they have to take themselves so seriously all the time?!

Me and the rest of our cabin made our way to the benches at the side of the stage and picked up our instruments, while Phoebe and the other girls got into their starting positions on stage. The sports hall was dead silent, waiting for us to begin.

Miss Moulson started the backing track and the WPC girls began to throw themselves about. The more I watched them, enjoying being the centre of attention while we were sitting on a bench playing percussion, the angrier I got.

How dare she drop marshmallow in my hair?

How dare she reduce me to playing the triangle?

How dare she push me in the lake?

How dare she read my diary?

How dare she embarrass me in front of Daniel?

How dare she think my toaster play was a terrible idea?!

Mark my words. One day she'll see my name up in lights and then she'll be sorry!!! Maybe I'll be so famous I will only be known by my first name, a bit like Kylie, Beyoncé and Adele!

The more I angrily imagined my toaster play being a roaring success, the more I lost concentration.

I mean . . . telling me I could hit the triangle only three times – how dare she?! I could hit the triangle as many times as I wanted!!

And so I did.

Have you ever heard of that saying '*March to the beat of your own drum*'? Well, I pinged to the beat of my own triangle! I must have gone into a sort of angry triangle-playing trance because the next thing I knew the entire hall was silent apart from the sound of me pinging.

Not exactly my most attractive look

The Slightly Awkward Potatoes were all staring at me like I was crazy, and Phoebe looked like she was about to cry.

Molly nudged me and whispered, 'Lottie, you can stop hitting that thing now. The dance finished ages ago.'

OOOPS!

So it turned out that the whole of Camp Firefly had been watching me angrily play the triangle solo for, like, three entire minutes.

The weirdest thing about it is that when I did finally put it down the whole place erupted into a huge round of applause. Apparently they thought my angry triangle playing was some sort of representation of the frustration and despair we all feel about the destruction of our planet . . . Who was I to tell them any different?! LOL.

Miss Moulson came over to the bench and took me by the arm. I thought I was going to get into BIG trouble for trying to sabotage the performance, but she actually took me to the front of the stage where I proceeded to get a standing ovation. You should have seen the WPC girls – they were absolutely fuming!

Now for the really funny bit. We actually won the Camp Firefly Cup!

When we got back to the cabin, we celebrated by having a massive pillow fight and an early midnight feast. Unfortunately, that coincided with room inspection (which we had forgotten about again) and we scored a very dismal 2/10. The shame!

THURSDAY 27 OCTOBER

Woke up to find that Mum had sent me a photo of the hammies. I miss those guys so much. They did look kind of traumatized though – I hope she's kept Bella away from them.

Today is our last full day at camp and I feel really mixed about it. I feel like we've just arrived but also like we've been here for ages. I feel like I'm looking forward to going home but also like I'm loving being independent and I want to stay here forever. Sometimes life is so confusing.

Good News 1: Despite winning the camp cup yesterday, the WPC girls are still really cross with us and are giving us the silent treatment, which is fine by me!

Good News 2: This morning we did archery, which was

fun because somehow I was really great at it and scored a bullseye.

Triangle playing, firing pointy sticks at a target, haunting people covered in sanitary towels – is there nothing I cannot do?!

After archery, we had abseiling, which I wasn't really looking forward to because I'm not great with heights and the tower looked super tall. I'd have rather done more archery, but you have to stick with your group, so I had no choice. Kai said it would be good to give it a try but, if I really didn't want to, I could just watch. That's what I like about Kai – he never makes you feel bad about yourself.

Jess, Poppy and Isha's group was finishing their abseiling session when we arrived, so we watched the end of theirs.

They were clearly having a brilliant time. Jess was on her final go and was getting ready to abseil down when Thomas (one of the boys in another group) shouted, **'OH MY GOD, SHE'S BLEEDING!'**

Jess got a panicked look on her face. 'What?! Where?!'

That's when I noticed that she had blood on the crotch of her light-blue trackie Bs.

I swallowed, suddenly realizing what had happened.

'Ewwwww, it looks like she got her period!' said Jason, who was in Thomas's group.

Then the group started to laugh and mutter, 'Gross.'

Jess had frozen at the top – it was so awful. I didn't know what to do to help her, but I knew I had to try.

'Come on, Jess! You can do it!' I shouted up.

She looked so sad up there, but eventually she managed to focus and get down.

When she reached the bottom, I helped her out of her harness and then I took off my hoodie and tied it round her waist – I'd never seen her look so pale.

Meanwhile Amber had gone over to the group of boys, who were still giggling.

'What's so funny?' she asked them, hands on her hips.

None of them could meet her eyes.

'I said . . . **WHAT'S SO FUNNY?'**

They started scuffing their shoes into the ground and muttering, 'Nothing,' but Amber would not let them off.

'How old are you? Five?! If you think periods are funny, then I suggest you might want to go back to primary school and do some low-level PHSE!'

They were totally silent after that and when Amber came back over we all gave her a high-five.

'That was epic, Amber!' I said.

'Yeh, thanks, Amber,' said Jess. 'I definitely owe you one.'

Kai gave me permission to miss the abseiling session (which I was secretly glad about anyway) so that I could take Jess back to the cabins. She had forgotten her period pack, so I took her back to Shooting Stars.

'I've been taking my period pack with me to school so I don't know why I didn't bring it on this trip. I guess I've been carrying it around so long that I kind of thought it might never happen,' she said.

'Don't worry, Jess. We've got supplies,' I said, smiling as I threw open our cabin door, revealing a room still covered in Always Ultra and Bodyform pads.

'Oh wow, you really do!' she said, laughing. 'But what –'

'It's a LONG story,' I said, handing her a couple of new wrapped pads from my suitcase. 'Do you need any help?'

'I think I'll be all right,' she said as she went into the bathroom.

I slid down the wall and sat on the floor outside, just in case she needed me.

'I guess I win then . . .' she shouted through the door.

'Win what?'

'First place for the most awkward moment to get your first period,' she said.

I thought back to my first period: I'd got it while dressed as a crab five minutes before I was due on stage for the spring musical. At the time I thought that was horrendous, but at least it wasn't as public as this.

I laughed. 'I will unfortunately have to hand you my trophy. Are you OK?'

Jess came out and sat down beside me. 'Sure, I mean, I *was* pretty embarrassed . . . but then I started thinking that those boys were probably only making jokes because they felt awkward too. And maybe it's a good thing that they saw the realities that women go through. Periods are just part of life, and we shouldn't be ashamed of them.'

I smiled and gave her a big hug. 'You are so right, Jess. We have nothing to be ashamed of at all. In fact, I think we need to celebrate. As my mum would say, *it's the start of your journey into womanhood* . . .'

She grabbed a pillow and hit me over the head with it, laughing. 'LOTTIE!'

'So how are we going to celebrate?' she asked when she'd stopped laughing.

'DUH – do you even need to ask?!' I replied, opening the snack cupboard/wardrobe. 'KitKat Chunkys, obvs!'

Jess grinned and we sat back down on the floor to eat them.

'Hey, Lottie, what kind of bikes do girls ride?' she asked, mid mouthful.

'I don't know, Jess, what kind of bikes do girls ride?'

'Oh my god. I think your jokes are worse than my dad's and Toby's,' I groaned.

'Come on. That's a massive ovary-action!'

I shook my head in mock despair, but it felt good to be spending time with Jess again. Bad jokes 'n' all.

6.45 p.m.

We are getting ready for the final-night disco. Everyone is v excited and our cabin smells like a perfume factory.

Luckily, while the rest of us prioritized packing snacks, Amber totally ignored the school's one-bag rule and brought two entire suitcases full of curling irons, hair accessories, make-up, shoes and a huge pile of clothes. Some people might call that shallow, others may say she's a fricking genius!

I managed to scrape mud off my best pair of jeans, but I was out of clean tops so if Amber hadn't come to my rescue I'd be going to the disco covered in pond scuzz. She lent me a cute pink cropped T-shirt and blow-dried my hair with a slight wave, then she finished the look with some Chanel mascara (!!), a shimmery blusher and pale-pink lipstick.

I'm really pleased with how it's all turned out and I'm mega excited to get to the disco, meet Jess, Poppy and Isha and have a good dance with them.

See ya later, potata! X

The disco was wild!

We wanted to arrive fashionably late, so people would be wondering where we were, but we were so excited that five minutes was all we could manage . . . In the end, no one seemed to notice us anyway.

The canteen, where we had been eating our lasagne just a couple of hours before, looked completely different. The bright white lighting had all been switched off, and now the room was dark, lit only by colourful disco lights. There was a disco ball hanging from the middle of the ceiling, and a smoke machine pumping out smoke that made everything feel quite mysterious and dramatic. I guess it was almost like being in a proper nightclub!

There must have been some sort of strange unwritten rule that all the boys should stand on one side of the hall and the girls on the other. The girls' side stank of Victoria's Secret body spray and the boys' side of Lynx. The smells met in the middle of the hall in a cloud of chemicals that made it difficult to breathe.

It was immediately clear that everyone had gone all out to impress. The boys were wearing so much hair gel that their hair looked completely solid like a Lego person's.

'OMG!' shouted Poppy. 'Have you seen who the DJ is?'

We all spun round and through the smoke we made out the shape of Kai behind the decks.

Amber practically melted on the spot. 'We have to go and dance at the front,' she said.

'But who will dare to cross the Great Divide?!' said Molly.

We looked up and down the hall and no one was budging. We decided we needed some sugar for Dutch courage so we bought Fantas and crisps from the snack stand.

'OMG – look!' Poppy pointed while shovelling salt-and-vinegar Chipsticks into her mouth.

It was Phoebe – she was crossing the dance floor to the boys' side of the hall.

We all looked on in horror.

'What's she doing?!' I asked.

'It looks like she's crossing the Great Divide!' said Molly.

'She can't just . . . walk over there like it doesn't even matter!' exclaimed Amber.

'She can . . . and she is,' said Jess.

We watched as Phoebe went directly over to Daniel and Theo and started chatting and laughing with them. Not for the first time, I wished I had the confidence to do stuff like that.

'She's dragging them into the middle!' said Molly, looking outraged.

Phoebe had taken the boys by the hand and was leading them to the middle of the dance floor where other WPC girls were heading over to join them.

'Oh, for goodness' sake,' said Jess. 'Who cares what Phoebe is doing? We're here to dance and have fun, right?'

She was so right! In fact, I think that was the best thing

I'd heard anyone say all day.

'You guys go for it – I'm actually here to stare longingly at Kai,' added Amber.

I raised my can of Fanta . . .

And so we danced, and we had an absolute blast. I seriously don't think there is anything much funner in life than dancing with your BFFS to Dua Lipa and Taylor Swift. It was especially good when Kai dropped a couple of Justin Bieber bangers and, even though the girls moaned at the time, I could tell they loved busting their best moves to them too.

Fifteen minutes before the disco ended, Kai turned the lights down low and said, 'Well, guys, it's nearly the end of the night and we are going to play some luuuuuurve songs, so if there is someone you've had your eye on, then now's the time to grab them for a slow, romantic dance.'

We all groaned. It was SO cheesy. However, I guess there were a lot of wannabe Romeo-and-Juliets out there because, despite the initial reluctance all around us, people started pairing up.

I started to panic. What if I was the only one left standing on my own?!

I didn't want to look over at Daniel because I couldn't bear to see him dance with anyone else. Part of me was hoping I'd feel a tap on my shoulder, and he'd be there, holding out his hand, but it didn't happen.

'Don't tell me if anyone is dancing with Daniel,' I whispered to the girls.

'Don't worry – we won't,' said Jess.

Just then I heard Amber. 'OOOOH, Lottie! Don't look over there . . . Pointy Nose has just asked Daniel to dance . . .'

'GRRR, Amber . . . I said I don't want to know!'

'OMG and he's said yes!!'

I couldn't help but turn round. I saw Daniel and Phoebe walking over to the dance floor, then she put her arms round his neck, and he put his arms round her waist. It was really horrible. I turned away so that I couldn't see any more.

Next, Theo came over and asked Molly to dance, then Dexter came over and asked Poppy to dance. Amber drifted off to do some more staring at Kai (apparently boys our own age don't cut it any more), and then it was only me and Jess left.

'Hey, want to dance with me?' she said, smiling.

Before I could reply, she grabbed my hand and pulled me into the middle of the dance floor, and we started dancing and spinning each other round. At first I was worried about what other people would think of us, but when I looked at all the couples shuffling around, barely moving and looking bored, I thought, *WHO CARES?! I'd rather be having fun with my BFF than doing that.*

Then I heard a voice say loudly right by us, 'Errrrrr, look at those lesbians!'

I was so cross!

I turned round to see Billy, a boy from Eight Blue, laughing at me and Jess. I decided to take a leaf out of Amber's book and put him in his place.

'And so what if we are lesbians, Billy? What's so funny about that?'

I suppose he thought that we'd be embarrassed, because he was totally lost for words. All he could do was look around, probably hoping that one of his mates would be there to help him out.

'Errr . . . um . . . I . . .' he stuttered.

Then Jess walked up to him, hands on her hips, and said, 'Using someone's sexuality as an insult against them is highly offensive and also . . . stupid.'

I gave her a high-five and for the next couple of songs we didn't think about Billy, Phoebe, Daniel or anyone else. We just concentrated on dancing and having fun, and it was the best end to the trip ever.

10.48 p.m.

OMG, how does this keep happening!?!? We forgot about the room inspection again and scored 1/10 because our room looked like a cross between TK Maxx, a beauty salon, a chemist and a dustbin.

Mr Peters said that we've had the lowest room-inspection scores he's ever seen in all his years of teaching – what an achievement!

(11.31 p.m.)

'Oh, come onnnnnnnn – one final haunting pleeeeeeeease!' begged Amber.

'Nooooo! I'm tired. It's been a long day and I just want to go to sleep,' I argued.

'But it's our last night,' pleaded Mia.

'Yeh, we have to do something,' agreed Ella.

'Well, why don't one of you guys be the ghost then?' I suggested.

'No one will do it as well as you, Lottie,' Molly said, grinning.

Urgh. They knew just how to get me onside. I rolled my eyes. 'OK, but I'm only doing it for, like, ten minutes, OK?'

Before I'd even finished my sentence, my cabin mates were already covering me with feminine-hygiene products.

(11.57 p.m.)

I have locked myself in the toilet. The girls are banging on the door, desperate to know what went on out there.

'Leave me alone! I need some time to process,' I shouted.

'Why, what happened?!' asked Molly.

'Come on, Lottie. You can trust us!' said Ella.

'WHAT HAPPENS IN THE WOODS STAYS IN THE WOODS!' I insisted.

'OK, well, we'll be waiting out here, eating your last KitKat Chunky, while you process . . .' said Amber.

'NOOOO!'

Don't worry – I managed to unlock the door, spring across the room and knock the KitKat out of Amber's hand before she could take a bite.

However, I also had to come clean to the girls, and now the room is silent and everyone else is just as traumatized as me.

So I suppose you're wondering what happened in the woods too, hey, reader? Do you really want to know? Because once you know, you can't unknow, and then maybe you'll wish you had never asked . . . Anyway, it's up to you. Maybe skip the next page or two if you are a little squeamish.

The night was eerie; the cabins were dark. There were no signs of life apart from the distant hoot of an owl . . . and of course a girl wandering about covered in sanitary towels. I was creeping up to my first window, about to knock and growl, when I heard a strange sound. A bit like someone whispering or moaning.

I spun round. Was there someone else out here? Was there a real ghost/mummy/zombie?! I was terrified! But I also knew that I would never be able to sleep if I didn't find out what that noise was – it was my duty to protect my schoolmates from intruders!

Slowly and quietly, I followed the direction of the noise. It seemed to be coming from behind a tree.

As I made my way over, my heart was in my throat. It sounded almost like voices.

'Oh, Philippa, you have such soft, sumptuous lips.'

WHAT?!??!?!??

I poked my head round the tree . . .

It was Mr Peters and Miss Moulson – kissing!!!!!!!!!!!!!! **URGH!!**

Unfortunately, I was unable to hold in my shock. I screamed loudly and they saw me. I'm not sure if they were able to identify me beneath my super-clever disguise, but I guess they might have spotted my trademark red hairband?!

I turned and ran back to the cabin as quickly as I could, trying hard not to vomit when I finally recounted the horrifying ordeal to my equally horrified audience. They were almost as shocked as I was. Mia looked like she was about to cry. Ella did cry.

'But teachers can't kiss, can they?' said Molly, her voice quivering.

'Of course they can kiss,' said Amber. 'They aren't robots!'

'They aren't?!' Mia spluttered.

'No,' I said sagely, 'and I'm sorry to have to say this, but it gets worse . . .'

The girls whimpered and clung to each other for support.

'Miss Moulson called him . . . she called him . . . Oh God . . . I'm not sure I can . . . I feel sick thinking about it . . . I'm just going to have to say it . . . SHE CALLED HIM "LOVE MUFFIN"!!!!!!'

Now we are all lying in our beds in complete silence. I don't imagine anyone will be able to sleep much . . .

FRIDAY 28 OCTOBER

(9.54 a.m.)

I woke up this morning feeling quite happy that we're
going home. There have been so many fun parts (and
some not-so-fun parts) but it feels like I've been away
for AGES and I miss my family so much. I can't believe
I'm actually saying this but I also really miss Toby. I
can't wait to be back in my own bedroom and for him
to burst through the door and fart on me. That sounds
mad – I know!

After breakfast, we had a chance to go to the shop to
spend the money (£10) that we were allowed to bring
with us. I bought a keyring for Dad, a jumbo eraser
for Mum, some sweets for Toby and a small, cuddly
teddy for Bella – she might be a bit young for it, as
it looks pretty flammable, but it's the thought that
counts.

Now we are back at our cabin and Kai has just been
over to say goodbye. Amber looked like she was about to

burst into tears as he left. He's been a really fun leader, but I think she is being *slightly* dramatic.

Right, I've got to go. The coaches leave in twenty-five mins and we've still got to pack and tidy the cabin, which is in an absolute state. None of us want to be stuck sitting next to Burger Tom!

(**3.45 p.m.**)

I'm home! I'm lying on my bed, snuggled in a duvet with my hammies, and it feels amazing!

After handing over my (very dirty) laundry to Mum (soz, Mum!), I escaped to my room because I HAD to fill you in on the journey home . . .

Annoyingly, we had to do all of Amber's packing for her because she was too upset over Kai to be of any use at all. She spent the time lying on her bed crying and muttering lovey-dovey quotes that I strongly suspect she was looking up on Instagram.

Because of Amber's uselessness and the fact that our cabin was one of the furthest away from the car park, by the time we got there I could see that the coach was already nearly full. There were little pools of vomit leading all the way to the door where Burger Tom was just boarding.

'Apparently the mere thought of getting travel sick is enough to make him travel sick,' said Amber.

'**Ewwwwwww,**' I replied, although I had to admit I did feel sorry for the guy.

'Lottie, don't look left,' said Molly suddenly.

'Why, what's –? Oh.'

I wished I had listened. It was PN with her arms around Daniel, planting a kiss on his face and making a big show of saying goodbye to him.

I sighed. 'If he's the type of guy to go for a girl like that, then I clearly don't know him very well at all.'

'Exactly,' said Molly, rubbing my arm. 'Now, let's get our bags into the luggage hold.'

I smiled and started dragging my case over when I suddenly heard a huge burst of laughter.

WHAT THE?!

I looked up at the coach to see a sea of faces in the windows, pointing and giggling uncontrollably. They were looking down at the ground. I followed their gaze and saw Phoebe lying face down in a pool of Burger Tom's vomit. She must have slipped while trying to show off with Daniel and it couldn't have happened to a nicer person.

I thought I'd be the bigger person and offer her a hand to help her up, but she told me to 'go away' (except using much ruder words). Charming.

'Goodbye, Phoebe. It was lovely meeting you,' I said sweetly, while stepping over her.

'Come on, girls! We've got to get going,' said Love Muffin – I mean, Mr Peters. Must get that right!!

When I glanced up and accidentally caught his eye, a strange look passed between us. He obviously knew that someone had seen him last night, but did he know it was me? I shuddered, put my head down and quickly climbed the coach stairs.

Unfortunately, by the time we finally got onboard, there weren't many spaces left. Ella and Mia took seats at the front, Molly and Amber grabbed the last double seat, and Jess and Poppy were already sitting together.

I looked around, trying to spot a seat with someone I knew, when I heard Daniel shout, 'Hey, Lottie. Do you want to sit here?'

He was pointing to the seat next to him.

The thing is, I really didn't want to sit next to him. I didn't want to hear about how his Wotsity hands had been round Pointy Nose's waist. URGH. I would have rather sat next to Burger Tom and been vomited on. But at that moment ~~Love Muffin~~ Mr Peters started rushing everyone to sit down and I didn't have any other choice.

I sighed and eased myself into the seat.

'Hey,' said Daniel.

'Hey,' I said, turning my back on him slightly to give him the hint that I really wasn't up for making small talk.

Then we sat in silence for about five minutes, neither of us saying anything. I got my phone out and remembered I'd not remembered to charge it so it only had three per cent battery life.

'So, did you have a good time?' asked Daniel.

As hurt as I felt, I couldn't just ignore him, and deep down I knew I didn't really have a right to be angry at him. 'Yeh, it was really fun. You?'

'Yeh, it was epic. Wasn't keen on that other school though.'

'Tell me about it,' I replied.

'Last night at the disco, the tall one with the pointy nose

grabbed me and made me dance with her to this really cheesy love song.'

OOOOH, this was interesting!

'Phoebe?' I asked.

'Yeh, I think that was her name. I had to run away from her in the end,' he said, laughing. 'She kept trying to kiss me.'

I laughed. 'I guess you can't help being so popular.'

'Coming from you, KitKat Chunky Girl,' he said, joke-punching me on the arm. 'What's with this hot French dude, huh?'

'Oh, that was . . . It was nothing.' Which was true. I hadn't heard from Antoine since I started ignoring him on purpose. He's probably so busy with his other seven or eight girlfriends that I doubt he's even noticed.

Daniel looked quite relieved. 'I guess it would be kind of hard to match my charms,' he said.

'Or your Wotsity fingers,' I said, punching him back.

It felt really nice to be back on good terms with Daniel again, but I suddenly felt quite shy and awkward too. What was I meant to say now?

I started fiddling with my phone for something to do and it immediately powered down.

'I forgot to charge it,' I said with a sigh, just for something to fill the silence.

'Want to listen to some music on mine?' he asked, offering me an AirPod.

It felt like a peace offering. 'Thanks,' I said, taking it and putting it in my ear.

Then he starts ruffling through his bag. 'I also have snacks in here somewhere.'

'I can't eat chewy sweets because of my braces.'

'Yeh, I remember. That's why I have these,' he said,

pulling out a bag of pickled-onion Monster Munch.

'I thought you said . . . they make your breath stink.'

'Oh yeh. I was just . . . I was just jealous because I
thought you'd met someone else.'

I couldn't help but grin. HE was jealous about ME?! Wow.

I reached into my bag. 'You won't believe what I have . . .
giant Wotsits!'

'But I thought the powder makes your fingers all cheesy?'

'Ha! Stinky breath and cheesy fingers – it's the perfect
combination,' I said, laughing.

He smiled. 'It really is.'

Then we both reached for each other's packets at the
same time and our fingers clashed in the middle. I felt
my cheeks go red and when I looked up I noticed that his
were too. But the weirdest thing of all is I swear a little
jolt passed between us . . .

I think it may have been a Spark ☺

When the coach pulled into the school car park, I saw Mum, Dad, Toby and Bella waiting there for me with the rest of the parents. They had made signs and everything.

I was so excited to see them that I gave them all a massive group hug and for once I let the Lottie Pottie slide. I didn't care if anyone else was watching – they are my family and I love them, and I always will . . . even when I'm a teenager! I PROMISE!

I can't believe that it felt great to see Tobes again, which is something I've never experienced before. (I wonder how long before I regret saying that?)

4.33 p.m.

I'm snuggled in bed and Toby just came into my room and did the most horrendous fart right in my face. It smelt like the sewers! VOM.

So the answer to the above question was approximately forty-five minutes.

5.44 p.m.

Got a text from Jess:

JESS: I forgot to mention it on the trip but me and Isha have another football match tomorrow. It's at Hove Park at 10 a.m. against Hangleton High. I mean, it'll probably be boring and you're probably busy, so obvs no pressure . . . but if you did want to come, then that'd be kind of cool xx

I didn't waste a second before sending my reply.

ME: I wouldn't miss it for the world!

JESS: THANK YOU, BFF!!! Xxx

Then I immediately messaged the rest of the gang . . .

ME: URGENT. You all need to meet me tomorrow at Hove Park at 9.45 a.m. Jess has a match and she needs our support!

MOLLY: Roger that 👍

> **AMBER:** Well, I am still feeling pretty crushed TBH but if I can stop crying for more than 30 seconds I'll try and be there 😭

> **POPPY:** See ya there xx

7.13 p.m.

The phone has been ringing on and off all evening. Toby keeps jumping up to answer it and saying, 'No thanks, we are not interested,' and then hanging up.

'What's going on with all the calls?' I asked Mum after the sixth time.

'Oh, we've been getting a few cold-callers lately – it's very annoying. Toby is just being helpful and answering them for me.'

What?! *'Toby'* and *'being helpful'* are not words you EVER hear in the same sentence.

This sounds V V V odd!

SATURDAY 29 OCTOBER

8.43 a.m.

My alarm went off at eight and I groaned. I think I could have slept for an entire week! Mum said that was a sure sign I was turning into a teenager, but I think I was just very tired from camp.

It feels so good to be back in MY bed again though. It's so much more snuggly and I've missed the aroma of my room, which smells like a combination of deodorant, Pot Noodle and hamster wee.

I mean, to you that might sound gross, but don't knock it till you've tried it, right?

One day I might pitch it to a perfume manufacturer and the hammies could be the mascots #FameAtLast

Amber just called to say that she's managed to get
out of bed and is going to make it to the game – yay.
Apparently she read online that chocolate helps heal a
broken heart, so she ate two large bars of Dairy Milk for
breakfast and now she can barely remember what Kai
looks like.

Dad's giving all the girls a lift to make sure we get to the
game on time – will report back later x

1.15 p.m.

OMG, that was epic!

When we arrived and made our way over to the sidelines, we saw that TSACG were already there and wearing their gang T-shirts. I sighed – why didn't we think to bring our merch?!

Poppy must have read my mind as she reached into her bag and pulled out a bunch of bopper headbands. 'I thought these might come in handy,' she said, smiling. 'And don't worry – I brought spares.'

We all put them on excitedly and started jumping up and down to jiggle them about.

'Hey, cool headbands!'

I turned round. It was Lola, Gemma and Sophia AKA TSACG.

'Thanks,' said Poppy. 'I had them made.'

'I love them!' said Sophia.

Gemma smiled. 'Yeh, they kind of put our boring T-shirts to shame.'

'Nah, I love your T-shirts,' I said. 'TBH, we were all a bit jealous of them.'

They laughed even though I wasn't even joking. I guess it did sound a bit bonkers saying it out loud. 'Do you guys want to stand with us?' I asked them.

'That'd be cool,' said Lola. 'We can all cheer Isha and Jess on together.'

And so we did. When the whistle blew to start the game, we cheered so loudly that the ref had to tell us to pipe down. The main thing was that when Jess and Isha looked over and saw all their friends standing there together, supporting them, they looked so happy.

And it must have helped a bit too because the Kingswood High girls won 6–2!! Isha scored twice and Jess got a hat-trick! I was the proudest friend in the entire world.

I mean . . . maybe they'd have done even better with me on the team, but it's their loss if the coach refuses to recognize my natural talent.

When the final whistle blew, Jess and Isha ran up to each other and had a huge hug. I felt a light flapping by my ear.

Angela.

Is it just me or does this cabbage never get the message?!

There was only one thing for it. I was going to have to get tough with Angela. So I grabbed her by her silly little wings and I threw her into the air and then I gave her a good hard boot!

Hopefully that will be the last I ever see of her!*

*Unless she's all chopped up on my plate** as part of my Sunday dinner.

**Although TBH I'd rather not see her there either, as cabbage is ewwwwww.

JESS: Hey, thanks so much for coming today. It was amazing to have so much support and it really helped team morale.

ME: You are SO welcome. You guys absolutely smashed it!

JESS: Thanks, Lottie. I do have one question though – at the end of the game it looked like you were trying to kick the air?!

ME: Oh, right, yeh. That was nothing. I was just . . . doing a few stretches as I got cramp in my calf.

JESS: OK . . . but you also seemed to be shouting something to someone called Angela?

ME: Yes. I call my right calf Angela. The left one is called Rebecca.

JESS: You name your calves?

ME: Yes. Doesn't everyone?

JESS: Um. No.

ME: Well, maybe they should. Right, I've got to go. I'm incredibly tired.

JESS: You were also saying something about a cabbage?

ME: I won't be taking any further questions at this time. GOODNIGHT X

Jeez, she should be a journalist when she grows up! Still, I think I styled that out pretty well.

SUNDAY 30 OCTOBER

10.55 a.m.

Tomorrow is Halloween and also an inset day, which is good because that means we will have lots of time to get ready. The Fun Police suggested that maybe I was a bit old for trick-or-treating, but you're never too old for free sweets and chocolate, right?!

I've been wondering what to dress up as for AGES . . . I wanted to do something really original but couldn't think of anything that wasn't going to be expensive or hard to do.

Luckily, Amber WhatsApped this morning to say that TQOEG had already planned our costumes and I didn't have to do anything – hurrah! I'm super intrigued to find out what they are . . .

1.34 p.m.

Oh dear. Mum has misplaced the Halloween treats. What a shame. I wonder where they could be?!

My official statement is that **I ABSOLUTELY DID NOT ACCIDENTALLY EAT A WHOLE BOX OF CELEBRATIONS** and, if she wants to prevent this from happening again, Mum should find a better hiding place for the Halloween treats!

MONDAY 31 OCTOBER

Happy Halloween! Today is the first year that I'm allowed to go out alone with my friends and I'm super pumped about it. They're coming round to mine shortly with the costumes. I've been trying to guess what they might be . . . Maybe vampires, maybe witches, maybe characters from *Stranger Things*?! Really, I have no clue.

Mum is taking out Toby and Bella, who are dressing up as matching pumpkins – OMG, Bella looks utterly adorable. Toby is not so happy about the whole thing!

Our costumes were amazing!! We went as angry triangle players!

We looked so strange and random that I think people were seriously freaked out. A couple of kids even ran away when they saw us coming, LOL.

Have you ever seen anything more terrifying?

After we'd filled our bags with treats, we headed back to mine. The plan was to watch a scary movie, but we couldn't agree on one that was scary but not *too* scary, so

we just stuffed our faces with chocolate and played the
Biscuit Face Challenge instead.

You won't believe this bit – me and Jess actually did it.
And the secret to our success? Party Rings, shiny side
up – result!!

TUESDAY I NOVEMBER

Back to school after what feels like FOREVER.

The worst thing happened in registration. When I walked into our form room, Mr Peters said, 'Morning, Lottie.'

'Morning, Love Muffin,' I replied. 'Oh no, I err, I mean . . . Mr Peters.'

MEGA CRINGE!

I swear that his cheeks flushed red – he must know it was me who saw him in the woods that night now. He didn't say anything though, so I just moved swiftly away.

Everyone was talking about the trip and retelling funny stories about the pantsing, the teachers' 'tea', the ding-dong ditcher, Pointy Nose and the mean WPC girls, the all-nighters and of course my outstanding solo performance in the camp concert. Tee-hee.

But the biggest convo topic by far though was the Ghost

of Camp Firefly – **MWAH HA HA HAAAA!**

Most people admitted to seeing a strange white figure walking in the woods, but they were undecided on whether it was a real ghost or someone playing a practical joke.

Some of the Year Eights have already started passing the story down to the Year Sevens, so it seems like the legend will live on, which I'm quite proud of. It's hard keeping it to myself, but, as Molly rightly pointed out, if I told everyone, then:

A. It wouldn't be a legend any more.

B. It would probably lead to me getting a detention, or worse still: suspended.

Today was also my first day in my new maths class and the good news is that I got to sit at a desk right next to Poppy, which was brilliant. Our teacher is called Mrs Vincent and she's really friendly. She explains things in ways that makes them much easier to understand. I already feel like my brain hurts a bit less than it used to, so I honestly don't know what I was worried about!

She set us some homework today and, as I actually understood it, I am almost looking forward to doing it . . . almost. I'll probably get Bella to check it all over before I turn it in though.

THOUGHT OF THE DAY:
Bit worried about this Mr Peters/Love Muffin thing! I feel properly traumatized by the ordeal. Am I ever going to get over it?! Am I going to keep getting his name wrong?! Am I ever going to be able to look him in the face again without imagining him and Miss Moulson behaving disgracefully behind that poor tree?!

STOP IT, Lottie, STOP IT!!!

WEDNESDAY 2 NOVEMBER

It's my birthday on Sunday and because of the school trip I've not had much time to think about it, so when my mum reminded me yesterday I felt a bit confused about what to do. Sometimes I wish I had a birthday in summer because that's so much easier – you can have outdoor parties, go to the pier, go swimming and all that.

The winter isn't quite the same, but I don't want to do a huge thing anyway. I figured I'd go with a classic sleepover, but when I told the girls at school they were like, 'NOOOOOO, Lottie! You need to have a party!'

I mean, I've never had a proper party before so maybe they are right, but also having a proper party makes me feel all wibbly inside because what if nobody comes?!

Amber suggested that I do something for Bonfire Night on Saturday. I tried to put her off by saying it was all a bit last-minute, but apparently the word on the street is that no one has plans and she reckons it would be really fun. Also, it would really help her 'get back out there' and put the recent 'traumatic experiences' behind her.

At dinner I told Mum and Dad about Amber's suggestion, and they thought it was a great idea. Dad started getting really excited about doing the fireworks and I had to explain that, although I'd like him to help with that part, I expected him and Mum to stay in the lounge for the evening and only come out when I have given them permission. They also shouldn't speak to anyone unless I tell them to.

So, anyway, now that's sorted, I designed an invite and here it is. What do you think?

M&D said that I could invite fifteen people, so I need to figure out who they will be. I'm going to give the invites out at school tomorrow and I'm even considering inviting some boys too if I can work up the nerve to do it!

Basically, I'm secretly really hoping that Daniel might be able to come, but shhhh – don't tell anyone.

PS Just to make it clear – I mean that I want Daniel to come as a friend, OBVS!

THURSDAY 3 NOVEMBER

4.22 p.m.

I gave the invites out to Jess, Poppy, Molly, Amber, Isha, Ella and Mia, and they can all come – yay!

Then at lunchtime we sat down together and tried to come up with a list for the remaining eight invites, but it was really hard because every person I wanted to invite led me to think of five other people to invite and it was hard to find a cut-off point, IYSWIM.

We'd been scratching our heads for ten minutes when Amber suddenly jumped up, grabbed the stack of invites and said, 'I've got a really great idea.' Then she ran off with them.

We were trying to work out what she was up to when she came back, clutching an even bigger pile of invites.

'What are you planning, Amber?' I said suspiciously.

'It's kind of difficult trying to narrow the invite list down to fifteen, right?'

'Yeeeeeeees . . .'

'So I photocopied the invite and now we have lots more – problem solved!'

'AMBER, YOU CAN'T JUST -'

But it was too late. She was already walking around the canteen, handing them out. I put my head in my hands, sighed, and then went back to finishing my cheese panini. Yes, my parents were probably going to kill me, but you can't waste a good cheese panini, can you?!

6.44 p.m.

We've been getting cold calls again tonight. Toby, as ever, seems to be super keen to answer them, which is highly suss as it's usually impossible to get him to take a break from his beloved *Minecraft*.

'Why do you keep jumping across the room like

someone's put a scorpion in your pants every time the phone rings?' I asked him.

'I'm just trying to give Mum a break,' he said. 'She deserves to put her feet up in the evenings.'

'Riiiiiight.'

Some people might buy it, but I'm not one of them. Maybe he's in some sort of trouble or maybe he has a secret girlfriend . . . One thing is for sure. There is definitely something fishy going on!

I agree.

7.35 p.m.

I called Amber for an update on the guest list and apparently nearly everyone she handed the invites to said they could come – great!

I asked her how many people she'd invited . . . She wasn't sure.

So I asked her how many photocopies she'd made. She said maybe ten . . . possibly twenty . . . or was it forty?

Certainly, no more than fifty . . .

GREAT!

Over dinner, Mum asked me how many people had
RSVP'd because she was going shopping to get the
hot dogs and buns. I couldn't tell her that Amber had
possibly invited half of Year Eight so I told her that I read
something in the news the other day about a big growth
spurt that twelve- to thirteen-year-olds go through that
make them particularly hungry. I said everyone was
eating LOADS at school because of it, so I said she should
get approximately triple the amount of sausages that
she'd been planning.

She looked at me a bit oddly but said she was proud to
hear I'd been reading the news. I just hope she doesn't
try googling it.

FRIDAY 4 NOVEMBER

I have had a nervous tummy ALL DAY!

People at school keep saying things like 'Looking forward
to your party, Lottie!' and that makes me feel even more
nervous because if they're looking forward to it and it
turns out to be **the worst party anyone has been
to ever** . . . what then?!

I'll probably get a new nickname at school . . . Something
like Lottie Bad Party and it will stick forever, and I'll
never be able to have another party again.

I don't even know what I'm nervous about . . . actually, yes I do. There are LOADS of things:

1. Nobody turns up.

2. People turn up but leave after twenty minutes.

3. The party gets crashed by mean older teenagers who get drunk and then trash our house.

4. My dad embarrasses me in front of everyone by putting on a slideshow of my naked baby photos.

5. Toby starts trying to sell guests his bottled farts.

6. None of the fireworks go off except one tiny rocket that makes a pathetic bang.

7. The hot dogs are undercooked, and everyone gets food poisoning.

8. I burn my hand really badly on a sparkler and have to go to hospital.

9. Daniel doesn't turn up.

10. Daniel turns up and kisses another girl in front of my face!

I honestly don't know why people have parties. It's much more stress than it's worth. If you're thinking about having a party, I'd just say DO NOT DO IT. It's the worst idea you will have ever had, and it'll only end badly, with lots of crying and potential hospitalization.

Is it too late to cancel?!?!

I could send out a mass WhatsApp telling everyone that I've been bitten by a diseased hedgehog or that my leg mysteriously fell off. That's not a bad idea, actually. Hmmmmmm.

6.04 p.m.

V cold. I've been sitting in the garden for two hours,

hoping that a hedgehog would come over and bite me but NOTHING.

6.23 p.m.

Mum opened the back door and shouted, 'What are you doing out there, Lottie?'

I said, 'Nothing much. Just waiting to get bitten by a hedgehog.'

'OK, darling. Well, tea will be ready in half an hour!'

I love the way that M&D are now so accustomed to my weirdness that they don't even question it . . .

6.29 p.m.

I guess part of the problem is that hedgehogs are pretty placid in nature . . .

Even if I end up coming across one, it might actually be friendly rather than bitey. I can hardly expect a hedgehog to be violent towards me without good reason . . .

So my next question is – how do you provoke a hedgehog?!

6.43 p.m.

Decided to stand in the middle of the lawn, shouting insults . . .

Now I just have to wait for them to come out and fight me.

Had to come indoors. The next-door neighbours were standing at their bedroom window giving me strange looks and I didn't want them to call the police on me again.

I shall have to revert to Plan B.

Just googled 'Can your leg just fall off for no reason?' – turns out it's unlikely to just 'fall off' for no reason, but I guess no one else will know that, will they?

8.25 p.m.

Right, I'm going to message the girls and put an end to this madness!

TQOEG WhatsApp group:

> **ME:** Sorry, everyone, but sadly the party tomorrow is going to have to be cancelled due to unforeseen circumstances.

AMBER: WHAT?! What unforeseen circumstances?!

ME: Unfortunately, the circumstances are that my leg has fallen off.

JESS: Your leg has fallen off?!?

ME: Yes, that's correct.

POPPY: Well, you had two legs at school.

ME: Yes, I know . . . It fell off on the way home.

MOLLY: How?!

ME: I don't know. It just . . . fell . . . off.

MOLLY: Well, how did you get home?

ME: I had to hop.

AMBER: You sound pretty casual about the whole thing, Lottie . . . Did it not hurt?

ME: A bit.

JESS: A BIT?!?!?

AMBER: Right, so where is your leg now?

ME: I had to leave it on the grassy verge outside Roger's News as it was too heavy to carry home while hopping.

AMBER: So, if I go down to Roger's News, I'll find your leg there, will I?

ME: Ummm, well, I guess someone may have thrown it in the bin by now . . . Look, can we please stop with the relentless questions. I think I'm still in shock.

AMBER: Oh, for goodness' sake, Lottie, stop being ridiculous. Legs don't just fall off outside a newsagent's! You're just feeling nervous about your party tomorrow, aren't you?

ME: No.

AMBER: Lottie . . .

ME: OK, yes. Please make it stop!

AMBER: It's going to be SO MUCH FUN! I promise.

MOLLY: The FUNNEST party EVER!

POPPY: What they said 👆

JESS: 🎉 🎉 🎉

ME: You'd better be right!!

Lying in bed feeling really bad about being mean to the
hedgehogs . . . I'd best go and apologize or I'll never be
able to sleep!

SATURDAY 5 NOVEMBER

OMG, IT'S PAAAAARRRRTTTTTTYYYYYYYYY DAAAAAAAY!!!!!

OMG OMG OMG!!!!!!!!!!!!!!

I'm not even going to apologize for OMGing too much because how often do you get to have your thirteenth birthday party??!?!?

Basically, only ONCE, so
OOOOOOMMMMMMMGGGGGGG!!!!

I'm still pretty nervous but also SO excited. I'm glad I let the girls talk me out of cancelling as I know I'd have regretted it.

I think everything is all sorted. Mum has got LOADS of sausages, doughnuts, crisps, fizzy drinks and hot chocolate and marshmallows, and Dad has bought a selection of fireworks and plenty of sparklers.

Toby has in his words 'made loads of helpful signs' and put them up around the house, but they aren't very helpful at all. Unfortunately, he is quicker at putting them up than I am at taking them down.

The only thing left to do is get ready and that's pretty easy because I will be mostly covered in warm clothes, a coat, gloves, scarf and bobble hat.

5.33 p.m.

One hour to go!

Dad's set up all the fireworks. Mum's put all the food out on tables. The garden is decorated with fairy lights, and we're going to put some logs in the firepit to help keep everyone warm. We also have a portable speaker so we can put on playlists – Amber says she'll be in charge of that or else I'll probably embarrass myself by playing 'that awful Justin Bieber rubbish or whatever cringe-fest music' I'm currently into. Harsh but probably true – despite her faults, I often think that everyone needs a friend like Amber!

OK, I'm going to go panic in my room for forty-five minutes before the girls arrive. They've promised to be ten minutes early so I'm not left standing in the garden on my own at 6.30 p.m., waiting for people to arrive.

11.07 p.m.

It's over! It's done and I've had my first proper boy/girl party and it felt really grown-up (mostly).

So Jess, Poppy, Amber and Molly arrived first as per our plan, and we all stood in the garden. I instructed them to do some chatting and laughing so that when other people arrived it looked like a 'cool party', IYSWIM.

Unfortunately, they weren't massively good at it, and the more I told them to relax and have fun, the more confused they got about what having fun actually meant.

'Look,' I said. 'Just stop overthinking it and act casual.'

'Now I'm even more confused,' said Poppy. 'What do casual people do?'

After a quick chat, we decided that leaning against things comes across as casual, so we tried that for a bit . . . but when you have five people all leaning against various garden foliage, furniture and ornaments the result is actually the reverse of casual . . . and just weird.

Especially when you try leaning against a gnome, like Jess . . .

Anyway, luckily the party began filling up, so we stopped awkwardly leaning against stuff and started having a good time.

I let Mum out in public briefly to help serve drinks and she was quite surprised by how many people there were wandering about.

'I thought we agreed on fifteen people, Lottie?' she said.

'Fifteen?! Oh, I thought you said fifty.'

'Please tell me you haven't invited fifty people?!'

'OK . . . I haven't invited fifty people.'

'Thank goodness for that! How many people did you invite?'

'Ummm, approximately forty-nine.'

'LOTTIE! What the –'

I made a quick exit at this point as Mum seemed to be getting a teeny-weeny bit stressed. I personally don't know what she was worried about. I mean, yeh, maybe there might be a little more mess than she expected but, seeing as hoovering is her favourite hobby, I'd have thought she'd be grateful.

Anyway, the main thing was that everyone seemed to be enjoying themselves. The only problem was that it was now nearly 7 p.m. and Daniel was still AWOL. I was desperate to go over and ask Theo where he might be, but I was worried that would look too keen . . . and anyway we are just friends so . . .

I felt a tap on my shoulder. 'Daniel?' I said.

'Lottie love, I wanted to ask –'

Oh, it was only my dad.

'What are you doing out of isolation?!' I demanded.

'Don't panic – I've not spoken to anyone, but I wondered if we should get the fireworks going? I don't want to leave it too late as we need to be considerate of the neighbours.'

'Yeh, I was just waiting for . . .'

'Waiting for what?'

'Oh, nothing. Don't worry, Dad – let's get them started.'

'Great!'

Perhaps Daniel wasn't coming after all . . . Perhaps I shouldn't have got my hopes up that we'd be able to fix things between us.

I said that Dad could make a few safety announcements but if he tried to do anything funny I wouldn't speak to him EVER again. He said, 'Oh, come on, Lottie – you can trust me,' and then elbowed me in the ribs and added, 'Or can you?'

OH GOD, I thought.

He walked up to the end of the garden holding a saucepan and ladle and then bashed them together to get everyone's attention. That's when I noticed he was wearing a cap that had 'Official Fireworks Technician' on it. I cringed – I wanted to die already, and he hadn't even opened his mouth.

'So, hello, everybody! I'm Bill and I'm Lottie's dad! Firstly, I'd like to say happy thirteenth birthday to my beautiful daughter! She's told me she'd rather I didn't speak tonight, so I thought I'd keep it brief but I've just prepared a teeny-tiny speech . . . Lottie was born on a cold November's eve at Brighton hospital. It was a long labour and she really didn't want to come out of her mummy's tummy. In the end, she had to be dragged out using a plunger-like device and for the next week she had a weird-looking misshapen head, which led to her nickname Cone Head.'

'OMG, DAD - NO!' I shouted.

'Oh, well . . . sorry, love, I thought –'

'NO!'

'OK, well, maybe not then. Could I just tell my joke though?'

Before I could answer, he launched right into it . . .

Dad then assumed that because no one laughed we didn't understand the joke, so he tried to explain it.

FYI to any dads who happen to be reading this: if you have to explain a joke, then it's not a very good one!

'Don't you get it? Because they're LIT – as in "lit" meaning cool, like you young kids say these days? Is that erm . . . OK . . . well . . . let's get on with it. Stand well back, everybody, and let the show begin!'

PHEW!

I grabbed a toffee apple from the food table and went to join Jess and the girls on the patio so we could watch the fireworks. I just really hoped that Dad would redeem himself slightly by doing a good display. Mum, Bella and Toby had snuck out to watch too – Mum gave me a little wave and I smiled.

And then it began. **BANG, BANG, POP, FIZZ** – it was awesome! I had assumed there would only be a few, but Dad had obviously put quite a lot of time and money into it. There were rockets and fountains and Roman candles. Everyone was cheering and oohing and aahing, and I felt myself relax. I smiled and took a massive bite of my toffee apple.

Oh no.

Immediately I realized my mistake. FYI: toffee apples and braces are **NOT A GOOD IDEA**.

I tried to pull it out of my mouth, but it was like the toffee had welded to my train tracks.

I jumped in shock when I felt someone tap me on the shoulder.

'Happy birthday, Cone Head!'

I spun round and came face to face with Daniel. I massively cringed for two reasons:

1. He must have heard my dad's awful speech.

2. Obviously, I still had a whole toffee apple in my mouth like some sort of medieval pig.

I had a sudden flashback to Amber's birthday party in April, when exactly the same thing had happened but I had a mouthful of mini burgers instead. Am I always destined to have an overstuffed mouth in front of Daniel?

I had to say something, so I said . . .

I mean, it wasn't exactly my best look.

Oh God, what was I going to do? I turned round and scanned the crowd for help. Luckily, my eyes met Jess's and she gave me a look that said, *Don't worry – I've got this.* She walked over, grabbed the stick and pulled as hard as she could until it came free from my jaws. Then, without saying a single word, she threw it over her shoulder into the flower beds and walked off.

And this is why Jess is the bestest BFF EVER!

'Nice toffee apple?' asked Daniel, laughing.

'Yeh, great, thanks,' I said, while trying to dislodge the remaining bits of toffee with my tongue. 'Glad you could make it – I'm sorry about my parents though. URGH, they are so –'

'Brilliant?'

'Erm . . . that's not exactly what I was going to say. Are you sure you don't mean embarrassing?'

'Nah. Your dad is hilarious.'

'You don't have to live with him!'

'Well, he's better than my dad, who barely smiles, let alone laughs, and he's right – these fireworks are LIT!'

I smiled – maybe Dad wasn't so bad after all.

Then we stood and watched the remaining fireworks. It was cold so I huddled a bit closer to him for warmth and he put his arm round me. It was so good to be friends again.

After the fireworks, we were all hungry again, so the girls helped me hand out the giant marshmallows and skewers so we could make s'mores over the firepit. S'mores are always my favourite part of Bonfire Night – we have them every year.

I like to get my marshmallow all crispy brown on the outside, so it's super melty inside, and then I put it between two milk-chocolate digestives – chocolate on the inside, obvs. Molly always makes s'mores with Nutella and chocolate-chip cookies, but that's too faffy and messy for me – plus, digestives are just the right size and consistency.

I saw Dad chatting to Ella and Mia. They congratulated him and gave him a high-five before he made his way over to me and the girls.

'That was amazing, Mr B,' said Molly.

'Ah, thanks, Molly – now I'd better get back to the isolation room before I do anything else embarrassing!'

'Dad, it's OK. Don't go. The display was amazing, thank you. Why don't you stay and have a drink?'

Toby comes bounding up to me. 'Can I make s'mores, Lottie, please?'

I rolled my eyes. 'OK then.'

Mum was behind me, smiling. 'Thanks, Lottie – he's been desperate to come out and join you . . .'

Bella – not one to miss a trick – saw her opportunity and made a grab for my s'more. She managed to swipe a fistful and gobbled it up in two seconds flat.

'BELLA BROOKS!' said Mum.

I laughed. 'Not bad going, having your first s'more at nine months old!'

Before everyone went home, Mum brought out sparklers. They may not be as bright or as colourful as the big fireworks, but I think I like them best – they look so pretty being twirled around in the night sky. We were all trying to write our names and make shapes and squiggles . . . and I may have imagined it, but I could swear that I saw Daniel draw a love heart . . .

SUNDAY 6 NOVEMBER
(AKA MY 13TH BIRTHDAY!)

11.32 a.m.

CRIPES AND WOWEEEE! I'M A TEENAGER!!!

I woke up wondering whether I would feel any different. Whether maybe I'd get a huge hormone rush and I'd wake up really angry at everyone for no reason. But, luckily, I still felt pretty much like me.

Although TBH I was dreading going downstairs, because I just knew that Toby and Dad wouldn't be able to resist making fun of me.

In the end, I was dragged out of bed via my nose – Mum was cooking bacon in the kitchen. **MMMMMMM**.

As I walked in, Mum said, 'Ahhh, it's my TEENAGE daughter! I knew the bacon would get you out of bed! Happy birthday, darling.'

'Thanks, Mum,' I said before turning to Dad and Tobes. 'Come on then – let's have it.'

They looked delighted. Clearly, they'd been rehearsing . . .

I couldn't help but let out a giggle. Then my eyes fell on the kitchen table, which was piled high with presents, all wrapped in different types of paper. There were lots of cards too and big, shiny helium balloons in the shape of a one and a three.

I sat down and took a glug of orange juice and got to work tearing the paper open.

THIS IS WHAT I GOT:

* New turquoise Nike Dunks – sooooo nice

* Mermaid hair curler

* A set of proper coloured pencils and sketchbook (with textured paper!)

* Four new books

* Victoria's Secret perfume

* Dior lip gloss – fancy!!

* Healing crystals

* Fart-scented candle (from Toby, obvs)

I was so happy with my presents that I gave everyone
big hugs.

Next, I opened my cards. Mostly they were from
grandparents, aunts, uncles and family friends – the best
ones had a tenner in them or sometimes even twenty quid.
In total, I got £85. Now, I just have to work out what to
spend it on. Decisions, decisions!

7.22 p.m.

Tonight it was my choice of where to go for dinner (obvs) so
I chose my favourite pizza restaurant. Mum said that I
could bring a friend, but I've seen my friends so much lately
that I thought it would be nice to hang with the family.

When the waitress came over, I took great delight in ordering
dough balls and an ADULT pepperoni pizza with EXTRA
pepperoni. I am officially too old for the children's menu
and there is nothing Dad can do about it – **HA HA HAAAA!**

It was probably the most successful meal out we've ever had as a fivesome, mostly because Toby took his iPad and I gave Bella my pizza crusts to keep her quiet. Mum got to enjoy her glass of wine, Dad didn't moan about how much it cost, and I just felt happy that everything in my life seemed to be working itself out.

When we got back home, there was another card on the kitchen table, addressed to me.

'Oh, that arrived while you were away,' said Mum. 'I found it in Toby's room earlier. No idea how it got there.'

I turned round to quiz Toby but he had already disappeared upstairs.

I looked at the envelope. It had a strange stamp on it and then I realized it was from France. *It must be Antoine*, I thought. I opened it – the design was a bit odd, but I was right. It was from him.

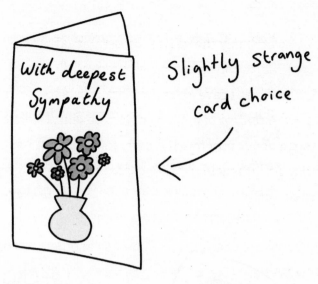

With deepest Sympathy

Slightly strange card choice

Inside it read . . .

Mon Cheri Dustbin,

Happy bloomin' good birthday to you, me old mucker!
Do I sound like an Englishmanfolk now? Ha!

I must apologize about the card. I hope you are
not dead or bereaved, but I sent my devastatingly
good-looking brother Hugo out to choose it for me
and this is all they had left in the shop.

Now to the serious part. Why do you ignore me?!
Why do you not return my 1.8 million calls down
the telephone line to yourself?! Do you no longer
like our chatty chats? Have you reignited your small
flame with the brown toilet deposit named Daniel?

When I call, Toby tells me you are in hospital because your entire body is covered in painful boils and every day the doctors have to pop them with pins and drain the pus. In one day they get five litres of pus – is it true?! I hope it is not true because I have dumped every one of my girlfriends and I would not have done that if I had been told about the pus boils – très horrible!

Please write back, you smelly warthog, and put me out of my misery.

Love of Antoine xxx

I slammed the card down on the table!

'TOBYYYYYYYYYYYYYYYYYYYYYYYYYYYYYYYYYYYY!'
I hollered.

I heard a giggle and a door slam upstairs.

I'm going to absolutely kill him!

MONDAY 7 NOVEMBER

Say what?! I'm down to my last few pages again! It doesn't feel like two minutes since I started . . . I'm sad to be leaving you again, lovely diary, but sometimes I just go on and on and on, and before I know it you are full up again!

Ah, well, as they say: all good things must come to an end. So let's say goodbye again with more of Lottie's Worldly Wisdoms (hey – that could make a good TV show!) . . .

Dear Lottie,

You are finally a teenager! It feels strange – strange but good. You are finally starting to feel more confident in yourself and understanding what makes you, you.

In case you needed any further clarification, here is a super-scientific diagram of your genetic make-up:

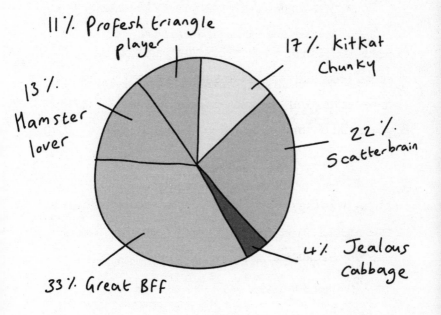

11% Profesh triangle player

17% kitkat Chunky

13% Hamster lover

22% Scatterbrain

33% Great BFF

4% Jealous cabbage

You've come a long way but, as always, you keep learning and growing. Here is some stuff we've figured out together:

★ You are a lot braver than you give yourself credit for.

* You can be independent; you can look after yourself and the people around you.

* You can do scary things (and often they aren't as scary as you might think).

* You can stand up for yourself and call people out when they are in the wrong.

* You love your family a whole lot . . . and maybe they aren't quite as embarrassing as you think.

* Your friends can have other friendships outside yours, but that doesn't mean that they value you any less.

* Being jealous is normal, but you need to learn how to manage it.

* *Finally, and most importantly, if you ever see a flying cabbage named Angela DO NOT LISTEN TO A WORD SHE SAYS. Just give her a massive boot right out of your solar system!*

Love Lottie
xxx

EVERYONE
IS READING ABOUT LOTTIE'S EMBARRASSING LIFE. TOTAL NIGHTMARE!

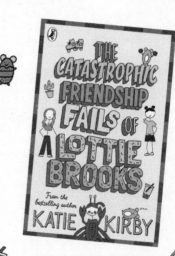

OUT NOW!

READ ON TO FIND OUT
WHERE IT ALL BEGAN...

THE EXTREMELY EMBARRASSING LIFE OF LOTTIE BROOKS

WEDNESDAY 11 AUGUST
(DAY 19 OF THE SUMMER HOLIDAYS)

Molly has only been gone for twenty-seven and a half hours, and no one seems to have any idea how much I miss her. It feels a bit like my insides have been ripped out, sloshed around in the washing machine, then stuffed back in again.

My parents are absolutely zero help. I guess, being friendless themselves, they have no clue what it's like to have your BFF move all the way to Australia. They just say stuff like, 'You'll make plenty of new friends in no time, Lottie.'

Like, how old do they think I am? Three? It's not like it was in preschool, where you'd just bounce up to someone and say, 'Let's do gluing!' then bond instantly over a shared Pritt stick. People are mean out there!

Here's an example of how my parents treat me like a kid: we just had drive-through McDonald's for tea, as a treat to 'cheer me up', and Dad tried to order me a Happy Meal! I mean . . . what was he even thinking?!

I did manage to negotiate a Big Mac meal for myself, but the annoying thing was that it just tasted horrible and dry and got stuck in my throat. Mum said maybe it was because my taste buds were finally starting to mature, but really it's because my heart is broken. I didn't even enjoy my milkshake that much. It had already melted a bit by the time we got home and was more milky and less ice-creamy than usual, you know? Then I got sweet-and-sour sauce down the front of my favourite T-shirt and it felt like the final nail in the coffin.

me

General aura of doom

sweet & sour

Anyway, with Molly off enjoying the sun and the surfer boys Down Under, I've decided to start writing a diary, and here it is. **TA DA!**

I guess it'll feel a bit like having someone to talk to over this long, lonely summer. I'm going to illustrate it too, because I love drawing cartoons. When I'm older, I'm going to be a comic-strip artist for a newspaper or a magazine. Might as well get some practice in while I have **NOTHING ELSE TO DO.**

Here is a picture of my family.

(Note: we don't all walk around naked. It's just that drawing clothes takes SO long and TBH I can't be bothered.)

I guess, as parents go, mine aren't *too* bad – that's if you don't count them nagging me about my screen time 24/7! My grubby little seven-year-old brother is another matter though. Man, that kid is annoying. Which reminds me . . . **IF YOU ARE READING THIS, TOBY, IT IS PRIVATE PROPERTY AND I WILL GET YOU!**

Hmmm . . . What else can I tell you about myself?

Ahhh, I haven't told you about my hamsters yet, have I? Here they are!

Professor Barnaby squeakington

Fuzzball the 3rd

Sorry not very good at drawing hamsters!!!

I've had these guys for about eight months now. They live in my room and they are a bit noisy, but I don't really mind, as they give great advice. Sometimes I tell them about how bad my day was and they just keep going round on their wheel and stuffing their cheeks full of food, as if to say, 'Don't sweat the small stuff, babe. There's plenty of bigger stuff going on in the world right now!' and they are so right. They always make me feel better.

Best not to ask about what happened to Fuzzball the 1st and Fuzzball the 2nd though. RIP, guys.

So, yeh. That's my life in nutshell. I've been almost totally abandoned in this big, wide, scary world and in a few weeks I'm going to have to start high school **TOTALLY ALONE**. Oh, and my name is Lottie Brooks. And I live by the sea in Brighton, in the UK. And I'm eleven and three quarters. I guess you might like to know that too.

KATIE KIRBY is a writer and illustrator who lives by the sea in Hove with her husband, two sons and dog Sasha.

She has a degree in advertising and marketing, and after spending several years working in London media agencies, which basically involved hanging out in fancy restaurants and pretending to know what she was talking about, she had some children and decided to start a blog called 'Hurrah for Gin' about the gross injustice of it all.

Many people said her sense of humour was silly and immature, so she is now having a bash at writing children's fiction.

Katie likes gin, rabbits, overthinking things, the smell of launderettes and Monster Munch. She does not like losing at board games or writing about herself in the third person.